Anna Cuffaro

BRITANNIA RULES

Published through *lulu.com*

International edition first published January 2006

1..3

ISBN-10:   1-4116-7077-9

ISBN-13:   978-1-4116-7077-8

Visit our website *www.britanniarules.co.uk*

The quotation from Evelyn Waugh's <u>Decline and Fall</u> is reproduced by permission of Penguin Books Ltd.

Dedicated to David, Daniele and Rosangela

Anna Cuffaro is a teacher and translator.

Many thanks to:

David Kauders for tremendous support and encouragement with the book.

Daniele Cuffaro and Rosangela Cuffaro for constructive criticism and for listening to me patiently while I went on about the book. A special thanks to Rosangela for designing the front cover.

Philip Mosely, David Myddelton and Martin Griffin for reading the book before publication and for providing me with their valuable comments.

Abbreviations:

ASBO	Anti-Social Behaviour Order
ADD	Attention Deficit Disorder
AP	Assistant Principal
AS	First part of pre-university examination *(age 16 to 17, Year 12)*
CRB	Criminal Records Bureau
DfES	department for education and skills
GTCE	General Teaching Council for England
LEA	Local education authority *(usually a county or unitary council)*
NUT	National Union of Teachers
OAP	Old Age Pensioner
OECD	Organisation for Economic Co-operation and Development
OFSTED	Office for Standards in Education
P45	Tax form given to job leavers in UK
PE	Physical Education (sport)
PGCE	Post Graduate Certificate in Education *(a teaching qualification)*
PISA	Programme for International Student Assessment
QCA	Qualifications and Curriculum Agency
QTS	Qualified Teacher Status
TES	Times Educational Supplement
tda	training and development agency for schools *(previously TTA – Teacher Training Agency)*

For readers outside the United Kingdom:

catchment area
A precise locality from which a state school draws its pupils

council estate
Housing provided at public expense and rented out by local government

GCSE
General Certificate of Secondary Education *(School-leaving certificate)*
The exam is usually taken at 16 years old

Graduate Teacher Programme
Alternative qualification, training and working interspersed

Key Stages 1 to 4
Division into age groups of compulsory education

Spin
Draw out and twist ... tell a story ... be in a whirl through dizziness or astonishment *(Oxford English Dictionary)*

Spin doctor
A political spokesperson employed to give a favourable interpretation of events to the media *(Oxford English Dictionary)*

Years 7 to 11
Secondary school years (ages 11 to 16)

The following terms have been created especially for Britannia Rules:

BPP	Blank Page Phobia, see Chapter 11
Bureaulish	See Chapter 11 (also Bureauland, where it is spoken)
DCRR	Daydreaming Clip Reality Regained, see Chapter 35
JIS	Jargon Imposed by the State, see Chapter 13
MPD	Mad Paper Disease, see Chapter 11

I was born and brought up in England. After leaving England, over twenty years ago, I took the place around with me. Now I can see that I got caught up in a time-warp in that I thought the country was still that which I had loved as a child and young person. Little did I know that Britain had undergone so much change that, when I came back, I could hardly recognise the country I had grown up in. It was a cultural shock - between the culture I had known before and as it is now. And the change was not for the better.

The tone of this book is light and critical. It might even be considered irreverent by some. All I can add is that I tell events as I perceived them and through my personality. I saw some of the mechanisms I came in contact with as absurd, and the outcome was that of anger and sadness. Maybe for people who have never left, changes crept up on them and they hardly noticed what was happening. It's difficult for me to judge - all I can do is to tell my story.

Switzerland, January 2006

" 'We class schools, you see, into four grades: Leading School, First-rate School, Good School, and School. Frankly,' said Mr. Levy, 'School is pretty bad ...' "
<u>Decline and Fall</u> (1928) Evelyn Waugh (1903-66)

1

Before I returned to England, I had already found a job as Teacher of English in a Comprehensive. It was only after I had been at the Comprehensive for a week that I found out that the school, as it was, had been closed and re-opened under a new name because of its lurid past which had made the national newspapers. Of course, having lived on the continent for over twenty years, I walked into the job without knowing anything about this episode. The school was obviously seeking to rub this heinous mark off itself, and the management was desperately preparing to pass the imminent OFSTED inspection.

I found out that the laughable feature about closing schools down was that they re-open under another name like this one had. However, some of those people who had contributed to the closure, seemed to remain firmly in place, or even promoted. I didn't find that logical at all. But, I was soon to find out that logic is not a priority in the workings of English education. Giving schools a new name, or a merger, is usually a sign that the school has failed the OFSTED inspection and has to "re-open", and hence start "afresh" under a new guise!

New headteachers are brought in and placed at the helm of a failing school. The headteacher, though, will probably be confronted with a ready-made ancien régime, set in its ways. Because the headteacher is a newcomer, s/he will need the collaboration of entrenched middle-management to settle in and to get to grips with the place. Entrenched management can ruin a new headteacher's chance of making a success of a school.

At this Comprehensive, the former headteacher had been brought in to improve the school because she had had great success in pulling a girls' school out of the pits. But this school was mixed. She had applied the same techniques here but had failed miserably. Given that this school was very different from her former school, a different approach should have been applied. She soon gave up and left for greener pastures.

I was interviewed by an acting-headteacher. She was the headteacher of a nearby school so took this one under her wing, too. When one is interviewed by an acting-headteacher, it is best to be wary of the school. During the interview, I was informed that I would need to obtain Qualified Teacher Status (QTS) in order to be eligible for the Qualified Main Scale Salary. I would have to start on the Unqualified Scale and go on the Graduate Teacher Programme. They would sponsor me in this, they promised. So I started on a bog-standard salary, although I had more than twenty years teaching experience.

Experience in education counted for nothing. Never mind that I had taught and been in college management, for over twenty years, and had a brilliant degree - these aspects were by-the-bye. The right bits of paper are obligatory, if you want to be paid decently. Management were quite happy to give me the job, and were confident I could work well, but they were not as felicitous to pay me properly for it.

When still in Switzerland, I received a brief email informing me that I had been appointed. The contract would follow shortly. Sending the contract heralded a series of messes. I received another email after a few weeks asking me to confirm that I would accept their offer. I hit the reply button and answered that it was indeed my intention to work for them. In that case, the school replied, would I mind signing the contract and returning it pretty pronto. But I did not have a contract! As coincidence would have it, later that day I received the contract. It had taken about three weeks to arrive. Secretariat had placed a UK stamp on a letter destined to Europe. I phoned the school and after some 'ohs' and 'ahs', with a subtext saying "Well, we are insular and can't stretch our minds to anywhere further than Dover", the whole incident was brushed off with a giggle. Secretariat was really proud about not being able to distinguish between UK stamps and European stamps. No-one had told them to adapt the postage stamps to different destinations.

Anyway, start at the school I did, with nothing less than the Induction day. A day of illumination decades after the light-bulb had been invented! The highlight of the day was the orange squash and pure orange juice. Not only did we drink it, but it also acted as visual metaphor. Much pouring of orange liquid, in its various forms, went on. We were asked whether we preferred squash or juice and to discuss the reasons why with one of the teachers sitting near us. I was agog. I found it so demeaning. Quite embarrassed, I looked around to see how the other teachers were reacting. Their faces were all serious. Like mine, I suppose. Gosh! How would all this proceed?

So, my neighbour and I conferred and agreed that we go for the squash. Reasons? Well, we would have control over it and would be able to water it down as much as we wished to get the taste which was most congenial to our taste buds. But, no! We soon discovered, to our utter dismay, that ours was the wrong answer. Good heavens! The right answer was pure orange juice. Definitely, the best in the teacher trainer's view, without a shadow of doubt. This was endorsed by the smiles of approval on the faces of her two assistants standing one on each side of her like columns. And to enhance her point the squash came from the "value" range, of a big supermarket chain, only 15p a bottle – cheap stuff. Contrastingly, the juice was some fancy brand. Our teacher trainer had not taken into consideration that some people might choose the squash. Absolutely out of the question. Squash was akin to pee according to our teacher trainer. My neighbour and I tacitly knew we could but shut up about our preference. She was a learning support assistant, and did not want to get into discussion with this intelligentsia of teacher trainers, and in front of a hall full of professionals to boot. And I, who hardly knew where I had landed, did not want to seem irreligious on my first day at the school. Pure orange juice it was then. So wonderful it was that the dynamic threesome decided that instead of calling the Key Stage 3 National Strategy by its real name (because it was too much of a mouthful), they would refer to it as Pure Orange Juice from now on. They slurped some of it down for good measure and then we were all offered a beaker full. Satisfied that they had got their message across, the session was declared over.

What's in a name after all? Call it by any other name, I thought, and it will remain as rigid. Key Stage 3 National Strategy refused to mix with orange squash and all the dangerous connotations it brought with it. Like, free- and critical-thinking, spontaneity and tailor-made taste; and last, and by all means least, saving tax-payers' money. Yes, all those people employed in designing the colourful and costly container in which the Pure Orange Juice is housed, would be traded in for a no-nonsense PVC bottle, with a Spartan label simply informing us about the contents and the price. As for all the squeezers of the oranges, they could sit back, file their nails, and let the teachers dilute contents in accordance with their own or the kids' personalities. The pantomime could have concluded with a good old shouting banter:
"Are all teachers the same?" "Noooo!"
"Are all children the same?" "Noooo!"

"Does Pure Juice keep the above two questions in mind?" "Noooo!"
"Is Pure Orange Juice flexible?" "Noooo!"
"What do we want?" "We want Squash! we want Squash! we want Squash!"

So I went home to sanity after a day which had proved an eye-opener.

There has been talk of extending the National Curriculum to the Early Years Foundation Stage. More precisely, this would extend from the age range of 0-5, that is: the newly-born, through toddlers to pre-school children. We could call this Pure Cow Juice. No doubt, Pure Cow Juice will have trainers drawing up theories on potties and dummies. Statistics might be published on the infant's frequency of peeing in the potty, as opposed to outside, and how many times, out of ten, the baby is able to aim its mouth, first time around, when seeking to suck its dummy. This data can be stored and linked to school achievement in later years.

2

The morrow saw the departmental meeting. On their first day at school, Year 7 would undergo a test so that streaming could ensue. We were told the procedure for the tests, and I was given 30 copies of the test for my class. At all times, we were to keep in mind that the kids had to enter the classroom in orderly fashion and had to be of smart appearance. Their blazers had to be kept on no matter what the weather, whereas teachers could continue wearing short-sleeved tops given that the heat was insisting on inflicting a sweltering late hot summer on us. The heat in some classrooms was overbearing but in the canteen it was simply unbearable. The sun's rays beamed in through the glass without mercy and bounced off the shiny metal tables. If one wanted a tan, this was the place to get it. The strong brightness could prove too much for the eyes though. You would either have to squint or wear your sunglasses. It wasn't senior management's fault if English summers had a reputation of usually being rather bland and no-one could survey a new situation and change the rules or hang blinds up in a short space of time just to make life easier. The sun had forgotten to give senior management ample notice.

Back in the classroom, I was armed with my pile of tests waiting for my enthusiastic newcomers to make an entrance. I was thinking that the lesson should have begun by now when, lo and behold, a small group of girls arrived.

"Is this where we're having our English lesson, Miss?", one asked.

"Well, let's see if your name's on my register, and I'll soon tell you. Yes, you're in here. Just sit down a moment. We'll wait for the others to arrive, then we'll begin."

But the others did not seem to want to turn up. After a while the door was swung open by a bolshie looking young lad.

"We got lost. Is this the T block?", he asked.

"Yes, this is the T block, and this is classroom 22", I replied.

To my dismay, I realised that the blocks in the buildings all carried Ancient Greek letters, which the kids were not familiar with. Perhaps senior management, in their race to pomposity to the detriment of clarity, had forgotten that Ancient Greek was not on the National Strategy Key Stage 2 syllabus? Some of my students had gone to classroom 22 in the Omega block, whilst others had simply wandered around aimlessly in total confusion.

The children kept trickling in now until I had more pupils than I had chairs and desks to accommodate them. At this stage, small clusters of them had mingled with the ones who I had already checked against the register. I'd lost count. I went to get some extra chairs from next door. When I came back with the chairs, to my horror, I found about another fifteen Year Sevens trying to get into Theta 22!

"You can't be in this classroom, it's full. Wait a moment, let's see. What's your name?"

Sure enough this boy's name was on my register. Then where did the others belong? The ones sitting on usurped seats and propped up at unrightful desks. Maybe they weren't Thetians at all. I was just about to panic when a colleague descended the stairs of Theta and appeared at the door to rescue me. Had she heard the hullaballoo down here? She made her way to me through the kids.

"I haven't got any kids!", she gleefully exclaimed.

"I think about half of these are yours. Does that solve your problem?"

"It might well do", she answered.

By this time, the laughter lines on her face had ironed out completely. So a sort-out began. We endeavoured to divide the children into hers and mine. Steady on, not so easy! The bolshie boy said "No". He wasn't having it. He had T 22 written on his letter and that's where he was staying. He had made himself at home, in the meantime, and didn't want to budge. His mate next door backed him up. By this time more kids were gathering behind my door in the corridor.
"Why don't you just take the ones who are standing up, and I keep the ones who have seats?"
"OK, let's do that. And we'll sort it out next lesson."

Needless to say that the 'entering of the classroom in orderly fashion' had gone awry somewhere along the line of the procedures. Some kids had even taken their blazers off. And the test? Well, we had to carry that over to the next lesson.

The confusion had arisen because secretariat overlooked changing the classroom number on the letters. If management had informed students that Theta looked like the London Underground symbol on its side, or had simply called it classroom Underground 22, life would have been made a little easier for my colleague and me. As it was, my classroom was quite Piccadilly Circus that morning!

3

The next lesson, there were still some lost little souls walking around Theta wondering which classroom to go to. "Are we meant to go to the first class we turned up at last week, or to the one we were sent to afterwards upstairs?" "Come in and sit down where you see an empty chair". This continued until all the chairs were sat on and the remainder I sent upstairs. The kids could be allocated to their permanent classes when the time for streaming came around. When the lesson was over, one of the English teachers appeared at the door. She had come to collect the scripts.

She informed me that it was her task to mark them all. How unfortunate! I asked how come such tedious business had fallen on her head. She started telling me the story of how she had got into teaching English. That's when I found out that those who can no longer teach PE, teach English. She had done herself an injury years before, during a PE lesson. As coincidence would have it, the accident came about at the same time as an English teacher had walked out, so she hobbled in to replace him. She had been teaching English at the school ever since.

Apparently, the chap who left had been utterly useless. That gave her the confidence to embark on teaching English given that it wouldn't take much to follow that performance. This year she had a group which would not even be considered for GCSE entry. She was teaching them to fill in forms. How practical can you get? This set me off thinking that in future, if the present trend of bureaucracy running savage in Britain is not reversed, these expert form fillers may well take over society. You don't have to stretch your imagination very far to envisage an eight-page-form coming through your door when you apply for a job, try to open a bank account, buy a house, take out a mortgage, take out insurance, buy your furniture on HP, and file for bankruptcy. Guess who's going to be drawing all those forms up in the future? And, when you are tackling one of these arduous packets, being able to recite T. S. Eliot's "The Wasteland" off by heart is going to be of no use to you whatsoever.

The PE teacher had actually taught GCSE, to Year 10 (14-15 year olds), during the preceding school year. As bad luck would have it, they had now metamorphosed into my Year 11 (15-16 year olds) and would be attempting the exam at the end of the school year. I hadn't met them yet, but already knew that I was in for a treat. They were the bottom group. She had been allocated the class last year because of her lack of a degree in English. I had been allocated the class this year because I was new.

It was thought that she couldn't do much harm with them. In fact, it is true that a good grip of the subject matter is not essential. Good teaching depends more on the technical abilities of the teacher. For example, you had to be able to write straight on the blackboard with your head turned towards the students, so that they wouldn't swear at you, or start hitting each other, while your back was turned. I had three problems with this. The first was that I had a frozen shoulder so couldn't keep my right arm up for long. The second was that I had eyes at the front of my head, and the third was that my head refused to swivel round 180 degrees.

The class had a reputation for being a rowdy lot. The next day came all too soon!

4

Year 11 strolled into the room in dribs and drabs. Lots of them! They couldn't quite make me out, viewed me with a little suspicion. They asked me a few personal questions. I told them I was born and brought up in England, that I was of Italian origin and had lived in Switzerland. They told me that they liked pizza, but they had never been to Sweden. One girl asked me how long I was planning on staying at the school given that most new teachers didn't last long. I said that the job was permanent, so I intended to stick it out. Surprising how forward looking kids can be!

As an introductory lesson, I thought I would start with a survey on what they had done. The most startling results. I found out that they had never done poetry. That had been unconsciously saved for me. They had no idea as to what similes or metaphors were. Therefore, I decided to defer teaching the effects of juxtaposition and oxymorons to a future date. They had, though, read Of Mice and Men with the ex-PE teacher. It turned out that before her, they had had a male teacher. According to some of them he was po-faced.
"You mean he didn't laugh a lot?"
"No, I mean his face was the colour of shit".
I pretended not to have heard "pooh-faced". When it came to clarifying homophones, they were very quick, only they didn't know

they were doing that. In choosing to use "pooh" in the first instance, they were merely being polite as they could have simply said "shit-faced" to begin with.

"He didn't teach us much, Miss".

"He kept going on about Shakespeare, and <u>Twelfth Night</u>".

As if teaching them <u>Twelfth Night</u> was easy business. I wondered how he'd managed.

" 'Cos that's all he knew, wannit", another answered.

"Can you remember anything about the play?"

"It's all about cross-dressers and poofs".

"You're a poof", one boy said to his next-door-neighbour. The latter thumped him one. After indignation over their behaviour, I managed to get them to move away from each other.

"Let's stop this carry-on, and get on with the discussion. So what else do you remember?"

"They take the piss out of their mate."

"Do you remember the name of the character who was made fun of?"

"It was the poof."

"Do any other characters come to mind?"

"There's a clown singing ponsy songs. Another poofter".

"Yeah, and then there's two brothers".

"No, one's a girl. 'Cos she's a lesbo, ain't she?", and the boy stuck out his tongue and started moving it fast from side to side.

"Well, it sounds to me as if you did learn something".

"Yeah, we kept watching the film".

"Did you ever read the text?"

"What text? What, on me mobile?"

"No, <u>Twelfth Night</u>, the text of the play."

"What do you mean?"

"Shakespeare wrote it down first then gave it to actors to recite. What he wrote is called a text. Texts are simply written pieces of work. You see, texts existed in Shakespeare's day, too. Only they were unabbreviated and much longer."

"Was they really much longer in those days, Miss?", snigger, snigger. Not content, he continued, "As long as a rocket, Miss".

General mayhem.

What about Of Mice and Men? What had they liked most about the novel? One girl answered that it was when he strangled the bitch. She added that anyone over the age of forty should be shot. Funnily enough, I would be included. I asked her how she had made the link between a young girl being killed and the targeted mass murder of all the middle-aged, and above, in England.
She answered: "It's murder, innit, Miss?". Rien à dire!
"What about your grandmother?" I pointed out assuming that her mother was under forty. "Would she be included?"
"Yeah, 'cos she's an old bitch and me mum's a slag".

What a double-barrel! What an ancestry! What a burden to take around with you! Had this gene run through the female line of her family for generations? Hadn't there been some soft-centred lass, somewhere along the way, who could have mellowed the future slags and bitches? Had the gene never skipped a generation? In short, hadn't the arrant knave of a gene ever been told to sod off?

But Miss Foulmouth wasn't the most frightening of the bunch. That prize had to go to a boy who hardly ever spoke and when he did you wished he hadn't. He sat alone. The dark, strong, silent and aggressive type. He had the look of a fuming bull about him, ready to charge any minute now. If there were a war, you'd definitely want him as an ally. Most of the kids kept away from him. Only a few boys talked to him and that was with reverence. He brought no school equipment with him; no books, no writing material, absolutely nothing. You don't need to hold a pen in your hand, if your fists are going to be clenched in your future career.

After I'd given the class some work to get on with, I hovered around him a little. Asking the kids around him to get on with their work, I slowly moved in on him. I asked if he was thinking of taking part in today's lesson. He didn't answer. "Get your pen out please, and I'll

14

give you some paper", I said moving towards the cupboard. I went back with the sheet. He left it there where I had put it. "I'll go and get you a pen, but I want it back after the lesson". I held it out to him to see if he would react by reaching out for it. Nothing doing. The pen had to be placed next to the sheet of paper. He made no effort to pick it up. He glared at me with a look which meant if I wanted aggro I had come to the right place. "You know what to do", I told him, "you have the material you need, all you've got to do is to get on with some work". My words fell on deaf ears. But his two worded answer travelled like a speeding bullet towards me: "Fuck off".

It has been decreed that children are allowed to swear at teachers, but only five times in one day. So that's alright.

5

I also had the pleasure of meeting Year 8 (12-13 years old) that day. There were quite a few special needs children in the class. Some were in categories I had never heard of. Some could neither read nor write. Because of this, they soon became bored, so indulged in much more exciting pastimes. I had never seen such a disruptive class. Children would get up, knock chairs over, break pencils and throw them at each other, tear bits of paper out of books, roll them up in balls with spit, then aim them at their friends, or put them down a shirt collar or two, if the victim was at arm's length.

The more artistic boys made paper willies. These guided missiles flew towards the girls with great hilarity amongst both sexes accompanied by pretence indignation by the shyer girls and appreciation or criticism of the size by the more brazen. Willies always got a good laugh. They are ever-present in the imagination of boys of that age. When I asked a class to create alliterative sentences, one in which every word begins with the same letter, I explained, one boy came up with a gem of reiterative and not so allusive language: "Willy, Willy, wound wound". That's when I made up my mind that for Key Stage Three kids, willies were Pure Orange Juice.

In moments like these, when one is slightly distracted, it is sometimes not apparent which strategy to use, there and then, out of the behaviour management rule book. Conscious decisions are called for in times of trouble and survival dictates acting fast. Rule 1234, control of voice. This rule has it that one way to control your voice is not to use it altogether. "Stand and wait for silence". I tried it. I stood and waited but silence didn't follow, strangely enough. How come it didn't work with this class? They just kept going on and on. "When you gain the silence required, the tone of your voice must be kept very low. The quieter your voice, the quieter the children will be". What was the contingency plan for silence not ensuing? If I had whispered in that uproar, they would have thought I was saying my prayers. They couldn't have cared less, they were having fun.

Following my intuition, I decided to have a good shout at them. This is regarded as primitive in rule books. No teacher worth tuppence ha'penny, shouted. That was not on. Only defeated teachers resorted to shouting. In theory, it must not be done. In practice, I heard just about every teacher bellow like hell, whether down the corridors, in the classrooms, or simply to each other from one toilet to another. Old habits die hard. By late afternoon, all the moisture in my throat had evaporated.

When I had finished taking my tutor group's end-of-day register, a teacher popped in to ask how things were going. I could trust him with the truth as I had first met him in the ante-chamber of the interview room. We were both waiting to go in. He had left teaching many years before to pursue a career in Media. He had been enthusiastic about returning to the chalk-face. It was only on Induction Day that we each found out that the other had indeed been appointed at the school. We had congratulated each other on our respective success. With hindsight, we would have gone into a long string of commiseration, but we were catching up on that now. Like me, he was surprised at how little practical information we were receiving compared to the useless information which was dumped on

17

us in reams. "Sometimes", he lamented, "I've got to ask the kids where we've got to go, and what we've got to do".

6

The school had two main means of communication. One was email, to which urgent messages were sent. Nearly every classroom had a PC. We teachers all had a school email address, too. Pity that I never found out what mine was. Even if I had known, it wouldn't have been any use to me because the system didn't work. One day, I witnessed the teacher in charge of the system getting rather irate with a supply teacher who had had the audacity of wheeling the PC from its privileged position at the front, next to the teacher's desk, to the walk-in pantry-like cupboard at the bottom of the room. "I'm sorry, but you can't move the computer", Mrs PC snapped. "There's nothing to be sorry about. I've already moved it so that proves that it can be moved for your information". I felt like applauding the supply teacher, but it wouldn't have looked good in front of the kids. She was so protective of her PCs! Her intentions were good, but they didn't start up the computer system.

The other means of communication was more user-friendly: good old fashioned pigeon holes. How much bumf Management could stuff into those little wooden boxes was nobody's business. Most of the hand-outs were printed on white paper. But because there was so much white paper in those boxes, anything that they deemed as essential reading would be printed on coloured paper, so that it would stand out. They hadn't yet come up with the idea of colour-coding bits of paper to suit the grade of urgency. They could have adopted the colour scheme used to warn people of the level of alert for terror threats, with black requiring the most attention. But then they would have to write in white! Whether white or coloured, Management was on a quest to rid the world of as many trees as possible.

One such piece of coloured paper was a reminder to resistant teachers, who hadn't been co-operative. These teachers had forgotten to fill in a white form sent by post before the beginning of the school year. The form sought information about which secondary subject teachers could offer at the school. It could be anything from touch-tapestry to how to look after your football boots. I had already sent my form in. I had planned to get into some story-telling - Greek Heroes.

But my form had 'got lost in the post', I found out later. That is, my form had not found its way to its rightful destination. So, I had to fill the form in all over again. Form-filling is a pet-hate of mine. I hadn't been quick enough to get my form back in the pigeon-hole because an Assistant Principal stopped me in my tracks in the staff room, when right on the point of placing the form back in her pigeon-hole. "Halt, stop", said her body language. "I suggest that you offer Italian as a secondary subject, Anna. A group of students is going on a skiing trip to Italy. Now wouldn't it be useful for them to have a little Italian under their belts?" She happened to have an Italian textbook in her office. What a coincidence! Why ask? She would place the book in my pigeon-hole. Goodbye Ancient Greeks!

Greek Mythology and Greek Tragedy are so fascinating. Greek Heroes open up new possibilities for us, and new visions of ourselves. In other words, they can help us to sort ourselves out. Very relevant to young people: "Who do I want to be?" as opposed to "Who do other people want me to be?" and the two contending together in "Who I am". The Greeks judge gods and their injustice. The Greeks ask the gods questions. "Why are good people punished?" and "Why are the unjust rewarded?" "Gods, is what you did to Oedipus right?" "Gods, you are not always right and you must justify your actions. I can create my own sense of justice which is better than yours, and I can even judge you gods. I will not accept your dogmatism and your absolutes. I can see what you are doing to us poor humans down here. I have learnt to think for myself, I am a free and critical thinker. You will not con me".

All this we had to give up, so that the kids could go and order a pizza and a coke in Italian on their skiing holiday.

7

The Media teacher also confided how shocked he was to find that the behaviour of the children had deteriorated so much since he'd last taught. "This isn't teaching, it's crowd control!", he exclaimed. Alas, how spot on! And, he told me about a few episodes he had been victim of that day. It is true that one of the most important aspects of teaching in comprehensives is behaviour control.

At a Comprehensive I taught at further along the line in my experience as a teacher in England, I was told of a teacher who had left teaching to join the police force. The experience she had gained while teaching at a comprehensive must have been most welcome in the police force. Anyhow, a police officer to patrol the corridors when lessons are in progress and in the recreation areas during breaks, would be money well spent. One less Pure Orange Juicer in Management, concocting airy-fairy theories, replaced by someone taking care of the more solid ground work. In fact, police officers have been placed in a number of schools across the UK in order to tackle crime and anti-social behaviour. This is a move in the right direction given that a lot of youngsters are out of control.

Teachers are at risk when dealing with unruly pupils. It is not unknown for teachers to be assaulted. The extreme case in which one teacher was murdered outside the school gates comes to mind. Teachers seriously risk being accused of assault. A colleague of mine was shocked to learn that I hadn't joined a teachers' union. She pointed out that if I were to be the target of malicious accusations of any kind, I could find myself jobless, financially ruined and even risked jail.

The Daily Express reported that the NUT (National Union of Teachers), which represents about 260,000 of the 420,000 teachers in England and Wales, said that 215 of its members were accused of assaulting pupils in 2004. This compares with 209 accusations in 2003 and 146 in 2002. Numbers are going up.

There was a case in Norfolk in which a distinguished maths teacher, of twenty-five years' standing, had been in court accused of assaulting a misbehaving girl. The teacher was suspended for twelve months while the case against him was prepared. Notwithstanding the fact that he was cleared, he still faced dismissal because the governors at his school had left that option open and he could not return to the school until they decided whether they would let him.

What did he do wrong? The schoolgirl was causing mayhem in the classroom by being cheeky and refusing to sit down, so he asked her to leave the room. When she refused, he took her by the arm and led her out of the classroom. What was he to do? There are no means of disciplining aggressive pupils which frighten them enough to make them behave properly. A lot of power has shifted from teachers to pupils. This inversion of tendency has turned out to be detrimental to the British education system. Blair's Labour government has even promised parents the right to contact OFSTED directly, if they are not happy with one of their children's teachers. Ironic, as it is usually parents who are responsible for their child's bad behaviour. And the government offers spin about respect and ASBO (Anti-social behaviour orders) ...

No wonder increasing numbers of teachers are leaving the profession in despair.

8

Back to our departmental meeting. The ominous OFSTED inspection looming over our heads took up a large chunk of the agenda. It was early September at the time, and the inspectors were calling in November. There was plenty of time to set action plans into motion. I was told that teachers sometimes practice the lesson beforehand with the students as many as four times. What a waste of time for the children. While they are repeating the same things they are not learning anything new. The head of English said, at the meeting, that if we had a lesson that had gone particularly well, we could repeat that when the inspector came to observe our lesson. Far better to tread familiar ground.

We were reminded that we needed to fill in all the right forms, tick all the right boxes and structure our lessons as OFSTED commanded. Only if we proceeded like this would we get OFSTED's benediction. Right enough, I started filling in all my forms. Every lesson had to have a plan and forms had to be filled in as regards the events which took place during the lesson. Everything has to be documented and everyone seems to be breathing down everyone else's neck in British education. There is a distinct atmosphere of lack of trust towards teachers. It is as if a teacher hasn't obtained anything unless it appears in writing or in statistics. What a contrast with Switzerland where the teacher is sovereign of the classroom!

The way the country is run is reflected in education. Spin buries the truth: failure at school is greater in Britain than in almost any other major industrialised country. In a study of the proportion of young people entering university, out of thirty countries the Organisation for Economic Co-operation and Development (OECD) found that Britain is below the OECD average. An article in The Times claimed that the "Education at a Glance" report said that Britain, at 48%, was well below the OECD average of 53%. The figure was 81% in New Zealand, 80% in Sweden, 73% in Finland, 68% in Australia and 63% in the United States. The UK has also dropped from 13th to 22nd in a generation for the proportion of young people with "upper secondary qualifications", equivalent to five GCSEs at grade C or better. Dr Andreas Schleicher, the head of the OECD's indicators and analysis division, said that Britain was being overtaken by other countries because standards of education were improving more slowly. The OECD found that the gap between educational haves and have-nots has widened.

The Daily Mail published the international league table of the number of school-leavers during the 1990s with basic secondary qualifications. The study confirms that since the 1960s Britain has dropped from 13th to 22nd place:

PERCENTAGE OF PUPILS AGED 16 WITH THE EQUIVALENT OF FIVE A* TO C-GRADES AT GCSE

1. South Korea   97
2. Norway   95
3. Japan   94
4. Slovak Republic 94
5. Czech Republic   92
6. Sweden   91

7. Canada	90
8. Finland	89
9. United States	87
10. Denmark	86
11. Austria	85
12. Germany	85
13. New Zealand	84
14. Hungary	83
15. France	80
16. Belgium	78
17. Ireland	78
18. Netherlands	76
19. Switzerland	76
20. Australia	75
21. Greece	72
22. United Kingdom	71
23. Luxembourg	68
24. Iceland	64
25. Italy	60
26. Spain	60
27. Poland	57

The obsession with league tables does not extend to international statistics. In 2004, like the preceding year, the English education authorities failed to deliver figures to PISA (Programme for International Student Assessment, of the OECD) maybe so that overall performance would not be revealed.

We might want to ask ourselves: how is the system performing? Is it capable of improving education? If international tables reflect a below average performance then Education is D grade in England. Who is responsible for this D grade education? OFSTED, tda, GTCE, exam boards, QCA, the DfES ... Will we ever know? If instead of sending a team of about fifteen commandos in to terrorise everyone and disrupt school life, if the OFSTED inspectors actually worked in schools, the inspector could report to a central office about the improvements s/he is actually making.

In other words, why don't they turn their theory into practice? At the same time, schools would need one fewer person in management. The salary saved could be used to take on an extra teacher. If managers are good, only a few are needed. As it is, schools are too top heavy. If the reports I have read in the papers are true, that only sixty percent of the money available for education actually gets to the schools, then there must be a great waste at the top.

For example, money does not trickle down to the photocopier. One day, a teacher nearly shouted at me when he saw how many photocopies I was making. He made me feel guilty because I had made one copy for each student. "No," he said, "they've got to share. Also, they are not to write on the sheets, so that you can use the photocopies again with another class". How ridiculous! In my experience as a teacher in Switzerland, it was considered positive to give students lots of handouts. It meant that a lot of work was going on. What's more, never did the students have to share, and they kept the copies, so that they could refer to them at a later date or re-read them at home. When management hand out piles upon piles of useless photocopies, that's fine. But, when it comes to the children, finances have to be watched. There is something wrong with priorities.

So it was that we lay in wait for OFSTED.

9

In the meantime, I wanted to find out why total silence had surrounded the start of my Graduate Teacher Programme. There were a grand number of Assistant Principals, or APs as they were called, in the school. Anything that moved which was a little more than a teacher, and less than the headteacher was an AP here. Pope John Paul II had appointed a record number of saints, so many that one wondered if they all fitted in the upper part of heaven. Similarly, headteachers invested power and glory on subordinates and elevated them to new-found pay rolls. In Switzerland, there was only one AP for a school that size. Furthermore, the role of head of department did not even exist! Unimaginable in Britain. So, how did the Swiss cope? Well, teachers are the heads of themselves. That is to say, teachers are deemed responsible and bright enough not to need someone to make decisions for them.

I started making investigations as to which one of the five APs was in charge of teacher training. As soon as I found out, as sheer coincidence would have it, she emerged from the top of the corridor and was coming my way. I stopped her in her tracks. "If you have time", she answered, "we could talk straightaway". So I followed her into an unkempt office. There were bits of paper everywhere, even on the floor. It seemed to me that the untidiness was a sign of confusion. In fact, my confidence in thinking her an expert was soon deflated. She didn't have a clue. She told me that she'd have to find out about it and would let me know. "But", I said, "shouldn't this have been organised before I started?" "Oh, there's plenty of time!", she exclaimed looking down her nose. She knew full well they were exploiting me. I got up, tripped over a pile of papers near the door, and left. From that day on, every time we bumped into each other around the School, she sought to avoid me. It was as if my wanting to obtain Qualified Teacher Status was getting on her nerves. A pre-condition upon employment was that the school would train me and, meanwhile, that I would work full-time for the school but on a salary paid to the unqualified, until I obtained QTS.

There was a lot of confusion regarding my status. My contract and salary indicated that I was unqualified. As for the rest, I was deemed an experienced teacher. As an unqualified teacher, I should not have had a tutor group, but one was dumped on me, without a question asked, when a teacher left one week into the beginning of the school year. To top that, I was also assigned bus duty and dining-room duty. Anyone would think I was qualified!

With a friend I started my own research about obtaining Qualified Teacher Status. Application had to be made to a university and the school would appoint a mentor. However, in order to get onto the course you had to have GCSEs in core subjects. One was maths! I had lived happily without the qualification until that fixed point in time and space, and I had told the school that I did not have maths when they recruited me. When I went to school, anyone who obtained as many GCSEs as most kids leave school with nowadays was considered some kind of freak of nature. On the other hand, GCSEs were not dumbed down then. One boy, Robert, got about eight GCSEs and he was the talk of the town. Core subjects hadn't even been heard of and now I had to have GCSE maths.

I hurriedly dashed to the AP's tranquil office to tell her my news. With a wide grin, I showed my face around the door. There she sat amongst her paper, so serene it hurt. She was not amused to see me again. Would they make provision for me to get GCSE maths? "No, sorry, we can't do that". That was totally out of her horizons. She had never done that before. How on earth could I expect her to arrange for a teacher to learn GCSE maths? Why didn't I just disappear, get on with my job and not go spoiling her day? My welfare was not her business.

I had discussed the Graduate Teacher Programme with the headteacher who had interviewed me. Now there was yet another new headteacher who probably wasn't aware of the situation I was in. My only hope now was to appeal to the good sense of the new headteacher and bring him up to date on the situation. Handsome and an awfully nice fellow. Would make an excellent impression on anyone. He had an aura of efficiency about him. Everything seemed under control. He gave me that "now-what's-on-your-mind" look. I got right to the point and lay my lament at his feet. He was sympathetic, assured me he would take the matter in his very own hands. "Don't worry, I'll deal with it personally. Come back and see me in a couple of days".

I let three days pass, just to be on the safe side. Feeling as if I were intruding on more serious business that the headteacher might have been involved in, I hesitantly knocked on his door. A very polite voice came back beckoning to me to "Come in". Sure enough he didn't have any concrete news. He had written to a university and would let me have the brochures and forms as soon as they arrived. They'd only take a few days, must be in the post right now. "But what about maths?", I exclaimed. "What about maths?", he asked. "Well, I've got to take GCSE maths before I can apply". After all, the previous management knew all about this back in May when I had been employed. "Oh, well, I'm sure you can do that without any problems, it's very easy". I had to lay this to rest and ponder over it

31

at the weekend before I said anything I could have regretted at a later date.

Like the AP, the headteacher had no idea!

So let's think this out logically. They didn't make any provision in May or over the summer. Didn't realise I needed GCSE maths to embark on the teacher training course. So what were they doing? Buying time or were they simply incompetent? As the grass grows, however, I was teaching perfectly well without the training course. The headteacher had complimented me after visiting my class and said he was receiving "good vibes". Unfortunately, the vibes which were making their way back to me were not of the same quality.

My friend and I decided that we would write a letter to the School and make a proposition. I could work part-time, pro-rata, and undertake the maths in my own time and at my own expense. The courses started the following week. I needed to have an answer soon because the evening courses were already full at the local college, so only daytime attendance would be possible at this late stage. A copy of the letter was given to the head of English from whom never a word was heard uttered on the question, either before or after the receipt of the letter. Silence. Not a rustle.

I had to press on with this. At the end of the school-day, I climbed the stairs to the upper chambers. This time the headteacher was standing in the doorway drinking coffee and laughing heartily with other members of staff. He had settled in. "Oh, it's all been seen to, the whole matter has been passed on to the AP responsible for teacher training". They were running round in circles. I toyed with the idea of swearing outright, but knuckled under to his authority. I smiled pleasantly and let my good sense prevail, thanked him and went home. My friend and I decided to draw up a letter stating that the contract had been frustrated as the school had dishonoured its undertaking to train me. I signed the letter, my friend posted it, and I didn't go back.

At the end of that month, my pay-slip came through the letter-box. It had the grand total of my whole month's salary printed on it. Were they going to pay me for the whole month? How could they be so careless with their money when it came to teachers? I thought no more of it, until one day I went to withdraw money from a cash dispenser and also checked my bank balance. From the total, it was obvious that no money had been paid in. What could have happened?

When I arrived home, I phoned my bank. Endless listening to options and pressing a great number of buttons, until I finally heard the voice of a live person on the other end of the phone, which startled me somewhat. After taking all my details, in case I was someone else and unrightfully gained top-secret knowledge of the millions teachers stashed away, I could tell her the reason why I had phoned before night fell. "So, you don't have a payment from such-and-such LEA (Local Education Authority) then?" "Yes, we do", she answered. "It doesn't show on my balance", I reiterated. "Just a moment, I'll pass you to someone else". So, I told the whole story over again. She had to put me on hold to find out what had happened. After a while, the lady came back to me and confirmed that the money had indeed been paid in but was withdrawn again. In short, Management had decided not to pay me.

At the same time, I had sought to get my P45 from the LEA. After conferring with her colleagues I was told, by the lady on the other end of the phone, that no-one knew anything about a P45 of mine. In fact, no-one knew anything about me at all. They had erased any evidence of my existence. I never did see that P45.

It was now my intention to take Management to the small claims court. My friend suggested I tried writing a letter to the headteacher before embarking on more complicated procedures. It worked. The

33

next month I received the meagre compensation for a throbbing headache lasting a fortnight.

10

In October, I went back to Switzerland for a week's break. While I was standing in the queue at security, I noticed a couple who seemed familiar. The woman kept staring at me, and I at her, until we broke the silence. I ventured "You look very familiar to me. Sorry for staring". "Oh", she answered, "aren't you the teacher who left our Comprehensive?" Of course, it was the Australian couple who worked there. I'm going to get a right ticking off now, I thought. "You did the right thing", she said and her husband nodded in agreement. What! Were there so many other people frustrated about the whole get up! Well, they certainly hid it well. We went through security and carried on with our conversation on the other side.

"Lots of foreign teachers are being employed now", she told me. "They exploit us. It's far more difficult for us to leave than the natives. At least we were together", she looked at her husband. "There are young women coming over who have to put up with it all because they don't know how to get out or don't have the money to go back home. It's difficult for them because going back means failure. Anyway, who would have thought that state education was such a mess in England? When we applied we thought we were going to a lovely well-run school. They're absolutely broke, you know. No money". Her husband was more concerned about behaviour. "I had children jumping out of windows and calling me all sorts of names. What can you do?", he asked. "Leave", his wife answered.

In fact, that's exactly what they'd done. They were going back to Australia with a few tales to tell similar to the ones I had. "You weren't the only one to go. Apart from the hard core, who have been there for years, teachers are frequently leaving and being replaced." She told me that the Media teacher had left a couple of weeks after me.

11

Off I went to a college to sign up for the GCSE maths course. Customer services confirmed that no places were free on the evening courses. Too late! I could either attend the two-year course on Tuesdays and Thursdays or the one-year course on Wednesdays and Fridays. The Wednesday and Friday course would be fine. I didn't want to drag out a course leading to a qualification considered a non-entity by most. Not having maths GCSE hadn't kept anyone from stardom. The following Wednesday at 14.45 on the dot I was sitting in the front row raring to go. I got quite excited about it all. The place brought back memories of my school days. The slightly decadent building, the stench in the classroom ... those were the days!

I was going on fifty and sitting in a classroom surrounded by teenagers younger than my own children. I did feel slightly degraded by it all. The youngsters were quite amused and wondered how I came to be there. I don't know how many times I had to repeat the events leading up to my being there. They still couldn't make it out. One girl said "But if you've taught for years, isn't that qualification enough?" "No, my dear, I answered, "you are young and innocent, the ways of bureaucracy are devious. Everything seems easy to you because you have not seriously engaged with the state yet. Mark my words now, one day you will understand and will not go making such haphazard remarks". A worried look appeared on her face. "Come now, my dear, don't perturb yourself unnecessarily. Maybe matters will improve in the future, though I doubt it will happen in your generation given that many people have been afflicted by Mad Paper Disease. It is difficult to cure and has now reached epidemic proportions."

For readers who have never heard of MPD, I will give a quick description here. MPD is an affliction that a lot of people have been overcome by. It is extremely contagious and rapidly spreads like wild fire. Once one is a victim of the condition, it is difficult to cure. One of the problems with curing it is that those afflicted are nearly always in denial. In other words, they refuse to acknowledge that they have MPD, indeed some do not even know that MPD has gripped them. It is latent in most and develops in certain environments, especially in stuffy offices where people sit close together. It spreads through words being breathed into the air. These airborne words, exhaled from an infected person's mouth, settle in another person's ear. There are two ways to stop the disease spreading. One is to wear earplugs because these impede infectious words settling into the ear lobes of susceptible victims. These words cannot then reach the brain and contagion is avoided. Some people are naturally protected from catching the disease as they have a built in antidote which comes in the form of common sense. However, this characical trait is rarely found in Bureauland.

One symptom of infection is that people begin talking in Bureaulish. These are jumbled up commercial words which find new combinations to create a language which seems learned to those in the throes of MPD but is actually utter rubbish. Just to give you one example, a spade would be called an "earth activating implement", rather than a "spade". This comes about because when a simple concept enters their brains, they elaborate it until it becomes obscure.

The afflicted are then overcome by the compulsion to see Bureaulish in writing. Hence the term MPD. They also develop a fear of blank sheets of paper, Blank Page Phobia or BPP, another symptom of MPD. It is eased by filling white sheets with Bureaulish, so develops into MPD. They never throw filled sheets away and keep copies of everything they write. When Jane or Joe Public asks for information, they proudly take one of each sheet off their shelves, stuff them into an envelope and post it to them. Sometimes Jane or Joe Public do not even need to make enquiries, paper will be sent to them without any effort on their behalf.

Professor Busk of Brainton University in Connecticut has been studying the phenomenon. He has seen huge rises in disease rates. Figures are expected to be out on Thursday. He will call for measures to combat the spread. In a chilling report which he has published, he states that we have only seen the tip of the bureaucratic iceberg. The situation is much more serious than it seems as many have gone undiagnosed. Also, the professor condemns the myopia of the government in not advising people how to avoid contagion as they continue to have frequent unprotected liaisons with the afflicted. He appealed to teachers to warn children by providing basic information and to protect them by teaching them to think. I quote: "Children who are instilled with common sense early in life, will be better equipped later in life to fend off the disease as they will be used to taking decisions".

One government official contacted by Professor Busk, promised that this will be looked into. He claimed that a Paperwork Reduction Committee was about to be set up along the lines of the American model. The PRC will organise surveys, draw up statistics, set targets, appoint inspectors, and open a helpline. A massive campaign will be launched. Information leaflets, including complaints procedures, will be sent out to the whole population.

* * *

I apologise for the digression which turned out to be longer than I'd planned. Let's get back to my adventures. I was relating my experience as a mature student on a GCSE maths course. The head of maths spotted me straightaway.

"Do you have a 'D' grade?", she asked out of the blue.

"Well, no, I don't. I've never taken the exam before".

"Then you can't stay here. This course is accelerated and you need a 'D' grade in order to keep up".

"Why didn't Customer Services tell me?"

"They are complete fools down there!", she exclaimed.

"Please would you overlook my lack of a 'D' grade and let me stay. I swear I'm quite bright and think I might be able to manage it".

"You will have to work really hard. Do you have ten hours a week for private study?"

"Yes, I do, I'm unemployed at the moment". For good measure, I added, "My friend's really good at maths, and I'm sure he'll explain anything I don't understand to me. My daughter has passed all her maths schoolwork on to me, she is also ready to help me work through the lot". My kids thought it hilarious that their mother should start a GCSE maths course.

"Have they told you the difference between a 3 and an 8 yet, mum?"

"Yes, I can tell the difference between an 8 and a 3".

"They look alike, but the difference is 5". Cruel sense of humour.

"OK", the head of maths gave in, "but don't let on to the others that you're not a 'D' grade". The youngsters were seeking to come to grips with their hormones. I was quite certain that they couldn't have given a hoot about a middle-aged woman's lack of a 'D' grade.

On Wednesdays, the lessons were conducted by the head of maths and on Fridays by her assistant, a young guy. During our first lesson, we were told that we would have to learn our times-tables, up to 15x15, and practice until we could fill the grid in under ten minutes. We would start with Handling Data. This module would be taken in November, so we had to get on with it. We started drawing up graphs and all sorts of charts. They were quite easy. Fridays were Inter-Quartile Range days. As the teacher came around to see if we had understood, he stopped to speak to one girl. She was part of a small group of young black women who were a little older than the others, maybe ranging from twenty-two to about twenty-eight. He asked if she had a 'D' grade. She said she didn't know what grade she had, an 'S', perhaps.

"How could you have an 'S', what are you on about?"

She retreated into her shell, went silent, and tried to get on with her work. She must have been making a real hash of her charts because he would not loosen his grip on her.

"Look I want to know if you have a 'D' grade or not! I'm sure you don't have one. You can stay now you're here, but you're not to come to this course again. It's accelerated. Do you understand?"

She didn't answer. I gave her a sympathetic look. It was soon break time.

That's how I came to make friends with the group of young black women. They were very friendly and shared their biscuits with me. It was through them that it brought home to me how down-trodden black women are. One hardly talked, as if she had given up, but she smiled a lot. Hers was a serene submission. Another told me she could hardly see beyond her nose, "I'm nearly blind", she told me. She was a single mother and unemployed. She'd worked hard to get qualifications in the hope of finding work. I told her I'd been unemployed for a few weeks. She reiterated that you think you are strong but that with time, the fact that you are constantly refused renders you unstable until you need psychological assistance. She had nearly given up finding work because every refusal started to feel like a stab in the stomach. The young lady who had been singled out by the teacher said she honestly didn't know what grade she had.

She was trying to improve her chances of getting a job and was also attempting GCSE English. Poor woman, could hardly have had much to write up on her CV. I offered to help them with their GCSE

English work and also helped them complete application forms for jobs. The following week she turned up again, and the maths teacher struck up the "have you got a 'D' grade" refrain with her one more time. She had a way of lowering her eyes to the floor and half-smiling which made her seem guilty in the maths teacher's eyes, but made me feel sorry for her and those like her. We had a replay of the whole tirade during the next lesson, the lesson after that, and after that again, until she didn't turn up any more.

The teachers in the maths department didn't seem to want students who weren't going to get decent grades. The head of maths had actually said "I don't want people here, if they are not going to get results". The maths teacher told one girl she might as well pack her bags and give up. This she promptly did. Only later did I realise that grades are propped up by excluding weak candidates from the exams. A lot goes on behind league tables.

12

When I wasn't thinking about maths, I was job hunting. I saw an advert in the paper for an Italian abstractor. I thought I'd go and see what it was about. "You never know", I thought. I had little else to do. The pay was abysmal. After more than twenty years' teaching, I couldn't really say that I didn't like my profession. As always, I didn't plan. I wasn't going to start planning answers for the interview. I'd take it as it came.

The offices were in an extremely plush building in the centre of town. I saw myself from every conceivable angle in the multi-mirrored lift and trod down the thick dark blue pile following the long and winding narrow corridor that led to their door. I was asked to please take a seat and was offered a cup of tea. The area in which I sat was immediately on the other side of the entrance door and shaped like a wide corridor. It didn't look as if many people worked there. It was very quiet. Finished my tea, a tall, slim Spanish-looking young woman with painfully short black hair came to collect me. She told me I would be given a test before the interview. I would have to translate and summarise a business news article taken from the Internet.

So I tamely followed her tracks, when all of a sudden, on my left, there ceased to be a wall and a vast open-plan office opened up. It was huge. It took my breath away. The only sound coming from the room was the clicking of keys on keyboards. There must have been more than sixty typists sitting there each glued to his or her respective computer. I was overcome with a sense of desolation. The feeling you are overcome by when visiting a graveyard. A feeling of sorrow for the waste of human lives. Each cadaver had its own flashing headstone. It contained data from when they had stopped living. Here was a place that rendered people comatose and incarcerated words. I could not be part of it. I was shown to a computer and started typing. No-one spoke to me. No-one smiled. There were no phones around. Just a collective clicking in disharmony. Is this what George Eliot meant when she referred to the muffled sound on the other side of silence?

The article was about a hotel development on some obscure island described as a holiday-makers' paradise. These places are created to give some sense to the boring lives people lead in order to earn the money to afford such holidays. Exchanging 48 weeks of this for a few weeks of that. I tried to keep my mind on the translation but was more interested in observing this gigantic typing pool in which people stared at their computers. Men and women all lumped together, mostly young. Sad how young people can waste their youth.

My train of thought was broken by the girl whispering if I would like to be accommodated in the interview room. My time was up. The room contained another lady who must have been the guardian of this cemetery. She was older than the rest. They told me all about the firm first. Then they speculated that I must be tired of teaching and informed me that they had quite a few disillusioned teachers amongst their staff. Mostly teachers from abroad who were sickened by the bad behaviour in English schools, or who had not accepted the heavy workload, or had come into contact with deficient management. Any one of these would be enough to make you turn your heels and head in the opposite direction from a comprehensive with the speed of a cheetah, but chances were that they had been frightened off by all three at once. Imagine what these poor ex-teachers must have been through to accept these working conditions. They had gone from the fires of Hell to this suspended state in Limbo.

The interviewers proceeded to work their way through their sheets by alternating questions between them. They came to the bit at the bottom which said "Ask interviewees, if they would like any clarification on any aspect of the aforesaid issues". "Would you like any clarification on any aspect of the aforesaid issues?", one of them asked. "When do you start? When do you finish?" It turned out that these people sat there eight hours a day. "Do you have any other questions?" "Yes, may I leave now, please?"

I had seen in the paper that there was a Recruitment Fair in town, so I made my way to see if opportunity cared to knock. To my delight, I saw that the Teacher Training Agency had a stall. There was only one woman there to begin with, so I had to queue to talk to her. She was speaking to a young man who wanted to embark on teaching but didn't have a degree. She told him that he should try to get his qualifications recognised as equivalent to a degree and then obtain Qualified Teacher Status. The slogan "Those who can, teach", towered above them.

I was next and explained my case. She reckoned that it was right that I should be paid the unqualified salary. In essence, the young man who was in front of me would be on the same level as me as soon as his qualifications were recognised as equal to a degree. I told her I didn't agree and experience should be taken into account. She suggested that I embark on a PGCE (Post-graduate Certificate of Education) course so as to obtain QTS (Qualified Teacher Status). A few people had gathered behind me by now. Though it hadn't mattered before, she was now overcome by an urgency to attend to them all. She thrust a leaflet on to me. I asked her if she had any

45

other suggestions. No, she didn't have any other advice. And that was it. Without further ado she addressed the next person in line.

13

Between job-hunting and maths, I would spend my days wandering around. One day I hit on a large car park at the back of some shops. After getting a few items at one of the supermarkets, I noticed a sign advertising that the building next-door was a college for adults. It turned out to be the smaller branch of a college spanning four sites. Nothing to do with the college where I was taking maths.

In Switzerland, I had been the Area Manager of a College for adults similar to this one. I used to teach at the College and was then appointed manager. In my area alone, we had about seven hundred and fifty registrations a year, in total the whole organisation had nearly eleven thousand students attending in a year. This College was much smaller than the Swiss College, only about four thousand registrations a year. I was astonished to see that there were so many people in administration here. What did all those people do? I was soon to find out that work can be expanded to cover the number of people working in a place.

Anyway, I walked into reception. There were two receptionists there, and this was the smallest site. I asked if they needed teachers. One of the receptionists asked me what I could teach while the other listened.

"English, Italian ..." I answered.

"Oh, we urgently need an Italian tutor. How wonderful that you should drop in! Could you send us your CV, please?"

I went home, printed off my CV and sent it straightaway. It wasn't long before I received a phone call from the head of Languages at the College summoning me to an interview.

The interview was at their main building. It was in an area which was notorious for drugs, prostitution and where shoot outs had taken place. A good idea to take education to where it's needed. One of the receptionists guided me to the interview room. The place itself was buzzing inside and brightly lit. We went through what seemed the heart of the College. A canteen in which lots of people sat. There were homemade cakes on a trolley near the hatch. Numerous green cups and saucers were scattered about on tables, interspersed with coloured chocolate wrappers. A busy and cosy place.

The interview at this College was to take place in a room just off the canteen among the dummies in the dressmaking laboratory. Some were partially clothed, the more daring were wearing nothing but their wigs. They stood there and partook in my interrogation by the dressmaking tutor and the head of Languages. Like at the Abstraction office, they too had interview sheets from which ready-made questions were fired at candidates. The head of Languages was new to her job, and the dressmaking tutor was there to fill a space. Somewhere in the instructions on interviews, a clause must have required that two people question the prospective candidate. The dressmaking tutor's free period must have coincided with my diary. There were lots of presences here. All as tangible as her and with an equal zeal for interaction. She asked me one question and that was pointed out to her by the head of Languages on the interview sheet. She nearly took it upon herself to ask another question without prompts but was stopped by the head of Languages before it was too late to expose herself as a free thinker. Some of the dummies didn't have heads. They weren't needed.

Kant's theory, on minors leading minors, was taken on board around here. According to Kant, maturity comes about when you have a totally independent and logical thinking mind. Though a college for adults, and run by adults, those who had reached maturity within the administration, in the Kantian sense, were cleverly kept from view of the public eye. They would surface, sooner or later, in positions of more importance. But the longer I was there, the more I realised that this was it. Everyone had to look up to someone, in order to function, and when the last one had looked up, they started looking down. The mannequins must have stood and stared with interest. They must have been holders of some memorable episodes in the history of English state education. If they had been created with the ability to make tea, they would have made ideal bureaucrats. Alas, that could not be. They couldn't get to the kettle, unless they were pushed to it.

Then I was introduced to their hundreds of bits of paper. It was at that point that alarm bells should have rung. But, I was so in need of meeting people and I sincerely love teaching. I have this innate passion for conveying what I know. I have this urge to share knowledge in the hope that students will catch my enthusiasm, then they will find a whole new world open up to them. But, no, more time was spent in filling boxes than filling students' heads.

A Lesson Plan (LP) was needed for each lesson. Why I've always chafed against planning and structuring, I couldn't figure out. It seemed to take the colours from the rainbow.
"We need to have the whole course documented. You must provide us with a plan for the whole course."
"I haven't met the students yet, how can I know in what way I'm going to approach my teaching without first getting a feel for the dynamics within the group?"
"You can make changes to the plans in the future, if you wish, but we do need these plans. Oh, and you must pay particular attention to respect ethnic origins and not to get into any stereotyping. Apart from

that, you must make sure no student makes sexist remarks. You know in some cultures knocking your wife every other day is seen as acceptable whereas we won't put up with that here." I thought I saw a contradiction. And then she added "You must state in your lesson plans what efforts you make to deal with diversity."

I had come across quite a lot of jargon at the Comprehensive. But this college for adults was even more wicked. In fact, the whole place teemed with it. For those who have not had the pleasure to come into contact with JIS (jargon imposed by the state), by diversity she meant disabilities and other differences like ethnic, gender, religious, etc. In short, we had to pinpoint how our students differed and write it down in a box allocated to this on our Lesson Plan. Not only. Given that we had to fill in a Lesson Plan for every lesson, we had to find something to place in the diversity box every single lesson. Next to the "Diversity" box was another box headed "Differentiation". To me it looked like a synonym of "diversity", but it couldn't have been because otherwise they would have merged the two together in one big box. It was only my fault if I saw sameness and couldn't diversify and differentiate between the two boxes by finding something diverse and different to allocate to each box!

Then I looked at the rest of the Lesson Plan. The first row of headings were for the Tutor Name, Course, Date, Time and Health & Safety Considerations. The second row were for Aims of each lesson and the Learning outcomes. The third row of headings was a little more tricky. Here you had to time each activity which took place in class and write it down under Timing (in minutes). For this I had to use the seconds' hand on my watch. To make it easier, I took my watch off during lessons and placed it on the desk in front of me. Some activities only lasted a couple of minutes. What a relief! I would have plenty to write in these boxes. Then for each timed activity, I would have to write the Teaching Point, Teaching Method, Student Activity, Resources and Assessment Method. At the end of the lesson, in the Evaluation box, I would have to write the name of

50

each student and comment on the progress made during the lesson. After the lessons, teachers are expected to dedicate a lot of (unpaid) time filling these sheets out.

I was offered the job and accepted. It was only four and a half hours a week, after all. Then, I was suddenly overcome by a frightening shudder. I looked at the interviewers first and then at the dummies. I kept looking from the interviewers to the dummies until I could neither differentiate nor diversify between them.

I tried like hell to look for diversity in my classes, I promise. And, I did triumph in weaning some out. The most important difference was that one lady was diabetic. I wrote in the diversity box "One student is diabetic". Because they wanted to know what action you took in the case of diversity, I added "She is allowed to keep sweets and cakes by her in case she needs them suddenly". None of the others kept bags of goodies by them, so that was different. That took care of one class.

The other class was made up of middle-class pensioners. They all looked and sounded quite English, but after scratching the surface I managed to find some differences. One was Scottish. In one of the boxes, I had to write the measures taken for celebrating diversity. We did refer to Scotland every now and then, and we also looked at how the Scots were running England. The other "foreigners" were of European origin, but they had been in England so long that they might have wanted to be regarded as English. I had to diversify them for the sake of my forms and in the teeth of EU endeavours of homologation. Vive la difference!

Which reminds me, one OAP got quite excited talking about a woman he had seen in shorts. I spotted some sexism here. I pointed out to him how we must discuss women holistically. Have readers noticed how some words become the vogue and are used whenever possible. "Holistically" is a word I would hardly have dreamt of using had it

51

not been for JIS. Did he try to find out what her IQ was? Did he look for other diversity apart from her tight shorts? No, of course he didn't. But, while they were in my classes, it was my duty to keep students on the rails of state imposed discipline of mind. You cannot notice one diversity without taking into account the other million and one diversities which make up a human being because you also have to be holistic. I must admit I did get my diversities and holistics in a twist on occasions. Perhaps I was trying too hard. Or, maybe I wanted to find out how far I could go before it didn't work anymore. I came to the conclusion that if you apply the rules one at a time and superficially, you're OK. But if you go into any depth, or try to apply rules simultaneously, you start to come up against contradictions. Contradictions are the basis of weak and collapsing theories.

At subsequent teacher training sessions, contradictions were plentiful. When the providers of educational wisdom are cornered, they will inevitably say that you should use your good sense on this one.

If they are imposing theories and rules on others, shouldn't they think them through thoroughly, too? And, of course, shouldn't they also have tested their theories so that contradictions are ironed out? The truth about new teaching methods is that none have ever lasted long enough to find out if they actually work. By constantly changing methods, the preceding methods are rendered useless. Teachers have to keep following the latest fad and are placed under punitive scrutiny by new strategies. Constantly overhauling educational methods, and imposing them, creates well-paid jobs out of very little. The international league tables provide proof of this.

14

The in-company teaching of Italian, on behalf of the College for adults, would be at a government office. The office was placed in an extremely busy part of town in the vicinity of an enormous shopping centre. Car parking spaces were impossible to come by in the area. The only way that I could get to the lesson would be if I could have a parking space in their car park. The 'no-can-do' answer was recited once more. The reasons were that it was too complicated to organise. In that case, I retorted I wouldn't be able to take the course on. I physically couldn't get from the office to my maths lesson in a quarter of an hour. It took them two weeks to get me a parking space for an hour when there were free spaces during the lunch break. I imagine that lots of bits of paper had to be shuffled around before the final OK was pronounced.

No sooner had I started the maths course and the College decided to change the lesson times to half an hour earlier than advertised. This clashed with the in-company teaching session I had just accepted to teach. I protested. They didn't care. 'No-can-do'. There was nothing left for me to do except to shift the time of the in-company class and have the lesson moved back half-an-hour earlier. This meant that the parking space issue was raised all over again! As the weeks went by, the students and I not only switched the time of the lessons but even the day to suit us. There were always parking spaces and apart from the participants of the Italian course, no-one ever noticed that we were not abiding by the pre-established regulations. The devils that we were, we had taken it upon ourselves to be flexible. Enough to make most bureaucrats cringe from the feet up.

15

Meanwhile back at the College for adults, I was to start a teacher training course. It turned out to be a hoot. Theory upon theory upon theory. We sat through endless boring evenings. One bright young spark asked if we were to imitate their (boring) teaching style. At first the teacher trainer didn't answer, probably thinking that he was taking the mickey, but then, she stated categorically that they should indeed be taken as an example.

The practice that did come about, all came from the teachers. We would, we were informed, have to prepare a micro-lesson which would be delivered to the rest of the class. This lesson should be the condensed version of an hour's lesson time. We were to actually teach, not simply recite bullet points. I raised the issue as to how difficult that was going to prove. I hadn't understood what exactly was being asked of us, nor had we been told how to approach this. I suggested that the teacher trainer gave us a micro-lesson, so we knew what it entailed exactly. She went red and I never did get to see the micro-lesson I so much wanted to be party to. The beauty about teacher training is that you don't need to know much about teaching as long as you have lots of theories. Ignorance about the practical side of teaching is an advantage because it only gets in the way of clear-thinking theory.

Then came the grand evening, during which two student-teachers showed us how to write up essays. This was done through the visual practical enterprising means of children's building blocks. "Now", said one of the teachers, "these bricks at the bottom", and she proceeded to lay them side by side until she had a fair-sized triangle on a scale of 1:30 of the real thing. "These bricks at the bottom are your base. They represent your introduction. The introduction must be solid. You must start your essay off with a bang". If there was going to be an explosion, I thought, it would be better to have it before the house was finished as this would save time, labour and money when rebuilding. No good completing the building, only to blow it up.

The erudite commentary accompanying the construction of Noddy's holiday home continued. "Now", she went on, picking up the primary-coloured cylindrically shaped bricks, "these are the columns". She placed them at even intervals on her base. "These columns represent your paragraphs. You can decide how many you need". I thought she'd need five for a house that size, but she reckoned that three or four columns would suffice.

When she came to the triangular bricks, a problem arose. What she needed was one gigantic triangular brick which would extend from the columns on the extreme left to the one on the far right. She did not possess such a brick that would do the job. Alas, she was without. If she'd had this piece then the whole construction would have bordered on the near-perfect. As it was, she'd have to make do, patch it up a bit. So she got hold of the rectangular pieces and carefully balanced them on the columns forming a row of bricks on which to stand the triangular pieces. The roof was now a series of roofs really, but we should imagine that it was only one big roof. And, guess what the latest endeavour represented? You guessed it. The roof represented the conclusion of the essay.

At this point, I wish to remind readers that the audience were teachers and not three-year-olds. No, they really were teachers at a training session. You see, in education nowadays, it is quite acceptable to apply the same teaching techniques from three-year-olds through to teachers.

The teacher then informed us that you could never write a good essay, if you didn't plan it first. Question time. "Excuse me, could I just point out that I've never planned an essay. I like to let my thoughts structure themselves as I write. That's how I worked all through my English degree". She threw her arms up and exclaimed that it wasn't possible. Essays must be built up and planned in advance like a house otherwise it would fall down. "Oh, my goodness", I thought, "to be that clever". I had bordered on a First in English at one of the best universities in Britain. The great irony of life!

The following week, the teacher's training course saw the distribution of little chocolate eggs upon entering the classroom. Great anticipation for the surprise toy inside. As if that weren't enough excitement, the non plus ultra came in assembling it. Like Hitchcock, the teacher trainer was an expert in suspense. She didn't give away the raison d'être of the eggs straightaway. This was a shrewd move on her behalf because she didn't want to influence what we did with the eggs. A psychological test! Yippee!

It was all about learning styles. These little eggs were the containers of such knowledge. What this teacher trainer could squeeze out of these eggs, right down to the last drop of powdered milk, was truly impressive. Put out of my misery, I soon discovered that the intellectuals read the wrapper first, whilst the pragmatists unwrapped the egg without worrying about the jargon on the wrapper, and shoved it into their mouths as soon as possible. Then there were the nibblers who read the wrapper while enjoying the egg. What were they? They were reflectors and were cautious. Someone came up with a good observation and argued that you wouldn't necessarily be an intellect if you read the wrapper because you could have read it on a previous occasion when you had bought a similar egg. "Hear, hear". "Yes,", came the answer of the expert, "but you <u>did</u> read it on that occasion". No-one, absolutely no-one, could waylay the teacher trainer.

Now, the teacher trainer was going to reveal the essence of our being, what stuff we were really made of. That all depended on the toy inside the egg. How would we go about assembling it? There lies the crux of humanity. I was, at long last, going to find out what made me tick. Forget Sartre.

"Would you tell me how you approached the egg?", the teacher trainer pointed to one of the students-cum-teachers.

After a little hesitation came the reply: "I looked at it for a while. Picked it up. Took the wrapper off and split the egg in two along its seams."

"You are conservative. You do not want to change the order of things".

The interrogated continued: "Then I looked at the plastic shell, First, closely, then from a distance. I brought it closer to me again and then twisted the top off from the bottom".

"You savoured every moment. You are ponderous", proclaimed the revered trainer.

"Yes, because I didn't know what was inside".

"What did you expect to find?"

"I thought it might be some kind of means of transport".

"What kind of transport did you think it might be?"

"Maybe a sports car".

"That means your lessons have a fast pace to them. On the whole, that's a good sign. But you need to be careful that you don't go too fast for some students. Not everyone works at the same pace, not everyone can keep up. Anyway, what was in your egg?"

"A little house".

"How did you go about assembling it? Did you follow the instructions?"

"No, I assembled it without looking at the instructions".

"That means you're impulsive. Not always a good thing in the classroom. Some caution is needed in teaching. You can't just assume you know what the dynamics in a classroom are".

"But you said I was ponderous before".

"Yes, but that was only on a superficial level. It was before you got into the centre. The centre is your inner self".

You could feel the tension rising as the conversation progressed at length. They got themselves into such a confused mass of intertwined threads, until it got so convoluted, that they reached a Kafkaesque conclusion.

While all this discussion from the deep was going on, I made an extremely important discovery about myself. I had taken to rolling the egg around on the desk making sure that it didn't roll off the edge of the desk by pushing it gently inwards, this time with my left hand and that time with my right, whichever was most convenient. What did this mean? I didn't want to know. I might have been considered superficial. Didn't take my lessons seriously. Indecisive, couldn't make my mind up, or unreliable, always to-ing and fro-ing.

My stream-of-consciousness made me think of the egg's symbolism. I'd been told during an Art course that it could represent fertility. The cycle of life going round and round, therefore, also a symbol of eternity. Yes, this lesson seemed to last an eternity, it was on the teacher trainer's lips and in her eyes. Could the rolling about of the egg have symbolised boredom, I wonder? The teacher trainer never did get around to analysing me. The fun we missed!

16

The day of my Handling Data exam arrived. I dressed for battle and, quick as the blowing of the breeze, in my imperishable shoes of gold, down I went shooting towards the bus stop.

The venue was a church hall. I was ridiculously early and waited upon the threshold of the courtyard until I saw a man in black. "Good day to you, sir". He kindly let me in, probably touched that at my age I should be forced to sit GCSE maths. This honourable place had put its hall at our disposal in order to secure God's support in favour of the examinees.

The flock was assembled, and the door of the lofty hall thud shut. We flung ourselves down at once into the chairs carefully laid out in neat rows. Then a lady spoke with bright eyes glinting. Hear me now, she ran through the rules. These words seemed a good omen and encouraged me. Praise be. She wished us 'Good luck'. May we be granted that blessing which our hearts desire. We were to sit two papers: a calculator and a non-calculator. One examinee didn't know she had to bring a calculator so turned up without. After much frantic ado, she finally decided to get her father to race down to the church hall with it. He arrived just in the nick of time. In God's house, the time was kept by an enormous great clock, the size of a chariot wheel, on the wall in front of us. We began on the dot.

Given that I hate being rushed, I decided to start off slowly but found myself gradually gathering momentum. I speeded up so fast that I finished before time. "Never give your exam paper in before time", is the examiners' advice, and "Always check through your exam paper meticulously". I touched the exam paper up here and there making it as neat as possible to the eye. Time was up. At last all this was finished and done. "All pens down, please!"

With self-satisfaction, I was leafing through the paper and simultaneously getting up from my chair, when, collecting my wits, I was horror-struck. I had left the last two pages of the exam paper blank. Two more pages of exercises lay overleaf and were completely and unambiguously empty. I bit my lips and thought "Oh, no!!" (I had loud thoughts). But now, it had to be given in as it was. I was helpless. Nothing to be done. No good appealing to everlasting God. My glow of self-satisfaction faded fast. My companion teenagers were sorry for me and were silent. Not one had the heart to say a word.

Humbled, I pointed my feet in the direction of home. I could have kicked myself all the way for being such a twerp. I phoned my friend. He reassured me. "If what you did was correct, you might have scraped up a C grade. After all, that's all you need". For the rest of the day I was in a foul mood until the sun set. Darkness came and brought relief.

17

A few months passed and I had almost forgotten about my maths results. I had switched over to the evening course with adults, which now had spaces available. Instead of mothering youngsters, I was now in a class with people nearer my age. This class was not taking the Modular exam. Therefore, no-one else had sat Handling Data. I was allocated to the same tutor as I had had during the day because he knew where I had got to. I asked my tutor if my results had come through. Sure, they had, ages ago. Not that I was told, of course.

I could go down to the office with him during the break and get my results. There before us lay a vast office. A spectacular sight. A mountain chain of paper. The indoor Alps. Paper, paper everywhere except hanging from the ceiling. A few piles were shifted and desk drawers opened and shut, so that it could be said they had looked. Computers had shut down for the day. The results were not in the office and, if they were, nobody knew where they were. I was told that I would have to go and find another maths teacher because it seemed she had a copy of the results. After finding her classroom, I waited in the corridor for her to come out during the break.

Sure enough, she had a copy of the dreaded list. I was haunted by my own face gasping with disbelief, eyes wide open fixed on those two blank sheets at the end of the exam. I gave her my name. She ran her finger across the page until she came to the column which contained the grade. "Erm, 'B'!", she exclaimed, "congratulations!". "No, sorry, that can't be right. Please could you look again. Are you sure that the 'B' is parallel to my name?" "Yes, I'm perfectly sure. You got a 'B', she assured me. 'B' was the top mark for the Intermediate Tier. Incredible. How could I score bull's eye, when I'd left out two whole pages?

The result was evidence of the dumbing down of exams so that more and more students obtain good qualifications. This is also true for A-levels. 2005 saw a record breaking number of high achievers. The mess created by drawing up exams which can be easily passed has brought about struggles for university admissions tutors to choose between tens of thousands of candidates with three or more A grades. A-levels have become little more than school leaving certificates. Because of these collapsing standards, pupils will most probably now face an aptitude test for embarking on degree courses so that universities can identify talented students.

Anyway, I was delighted with my result. Back upstairs. Climbing the stairs two by two to take good tidings to my maths tutor. This would knock him out. This will teach him not to have any faith in my mathematical powers. His difficulty in believing me made his jaw drop and his mouth open. The words got stuck in his throat and refused to come out. He found it difficult to formulate the words "Well done!"

Some students had been pushed out of the course by the attitude of teachers on the daytime course. Some came back sporadically for lessons. Tutors had to deliver results so, as a consequence so did students. One way of obtaining good overall results was to push out those who didn't stand a chance. Placing bets on losers is self-destructive. The better students at this College were usually people who were re-sitting. Here you seemed to reach your GCSE goal in steps. Step One: 'D'. Step Two: take the course all over again. Step Three: get the much coveted 'C', or above.

Having an adult audience went to our teacher's head. He raced on with the better students. Showing off his knowledge gave him a rush of adrenalin. Sometimes, his theories would even get too difficult for himself. He'd get into things he couldn't get out of. Then he'd say, "Forget all that", and simultaneously started raising his right arm to wipe the board clean. Then he'd swing his arm back down and add "Let's go back to what I was saying at the beginning of the lesson".

There were two reasons why we should "forget all that". The first and foremost was that that level of difficulty would not come up in the GCSE exam. The other reason, and by no means least, was that he had made a mistake. When times got really bad, theories might only concern us up to a certain point. In that case, he would have to go back, deconstruct the passages and tell us which bits catered for our needs and which didn't. It got so confusing that the best method for learning maths for me became that of forgetting all that I had heard in lessons, then going home and working it out for myself from the textbook. Eventually, I decided to take maths as a private candidate.

I was still attending lessons because I had to hand in two pieces of coursework, an integral part of the programme, which had to go through the College. One evening, he was writing the most obtuse algebraic equations on the board which only two people in the class could do. These people had been doing maths for so long that they couldn't remember when they'd started. It became an incestuous threesome. They went on and on, the two students in asking complicated questions, and then all three would explore different theories. Sometimes the students would tell the teacher where he'd gone wrong. Most of the other students sat silently trying to look intelligent. One brave woman said she had understood nothing. His reaction was to tell her she might as well go home for the benefit she was going to get from the lesson. I supported her and revealed that I, too, was clueless. He told me that I really got on his nerves. I had finished and handed in my coursework. The woman said she was leaving. I walked out with her. Given that we didn't finish the course, the College probably didn't get their government grant for us.

A couple of months later, I received a letter announcing that the College was now going to acquire the status of a university!

18

I was still looking for more work as the four-and-a-half hours' teaching a week at the College for adults afforded me the high life of travel from the kitchen sink to the washbasin and back.

The College I was attending the maths course at, had three posts vacant that I could apply for. I was told that I would have to fill in an application form for each job. They never as much as acknowledged receipt of even one of my application forms.

I began to wonder if they get government grants for the number of forms they managed to get people to fill in. Or, maybe it is good for their morale to see that they are receiving three times more application forms than their competitors. So three times over it was, then. Three times over right down to the next-of-kin details, bank details, medical information, that not even my best friend knows about, ethnic origins and just about everything you've done in your life up to that point. I must have written outside the allocated space because I never heard from them again. One of their slogans was "We are people centred". Yes, people were centred in the middle of big piles of paper.

Another job I applied for requested a CV. After I had sent that in, by return mail I received a tedious application form in which I was to repeat all the information they already had in my CV. There were also lots of other forms and an expensive colourful brochure. The brochure showed pictures of wonderfully happy children in Arcadia. Nobody cries in brochures, nobody pulls anyone's hair, and nobody's nose runs. Schools are represented in total felicity in an age of gold, without even a hint of a slight decline from an idealised state. Such is that pastoral dream that it is also woven into the brochure's artful prose. In brochures, comprehensives are a refuge from the complications of everyday life where everything runs smoothly. Unfortunately, the application form for Arcadia arrived the day after the closure date. So, returning the application form would have been useless. A couple of days later, I received a phone call from Arcadia's secretary summoning me to interview the next day. She assumed I was free. I wasn't.

19

As part of my job hunting, I had also contacted supply teaching agencies. I received forms back. I filled in forms for three agencies. Agency no. 1 asked me to fill pages of forms in. Upon receipt, they contacted my ex-employers and received excellent references. This I know because I had to help my ex-employer fill the forms in. It's like an English headteacher being asked to fill in copious forms in Italian. After the agency had received the completed forms and references, it decided that it required Qualified Teacher Status. So that was that.

Another agency had asked that I send a disclosure form along with the application form. I phoned the Criminal Records Bureau to inquire about disclosure forms. They required my address and also my credit card number or, alternatively, I could enclose a cheque when I returned the form to them. When I realised that every agency would require QTS, I decided to phone CRB back to say that I didn't require the forms. Too late! They had already taken the money from my account. "But that's ridiculous. I'm not going to send the form in, you will not be processing my application". The good ol' "no-can-do" was conjured out of the bureaucratic hat once more. This time with a view to keeping my £29.- for answering my call. They had taken the money and weren't giving it back, challenging me to speak to whomever I wanted in the joint. Even writing to head-honcho himself wouldn't make a difference, I was told.

They were there to make as much money as possible. Who do you go to when you believe that the CRB have unrightfully taken money from you? The police? I wonder if it is possible for the Criminal Records Bureau to get a criminal record!

"If I had said I was going to pay by cheque, I wouldn't have lost my money", I told him over the phone. They didn't want to see the logic in that. I asked for his name. He answered "Paul". They don't give surnames as this would nail people down. Every time I called, I spoke to a different person. I tried asking for Paul but heard a girl scornfully asking how on earth I thought she could find a Paul amongst all the people they had there - a needle in a haystack. "In that case, why don't you give your surnames or have an identity number?" She didn't know, it was no concern of hers. I asked her for her name. She answered she would give me her name later, but she never did. I asked for the name and address of the Operations Manager and that was it, Operations Manager. He must have a name! "Just address it to Operations Manager". I called again, spoke to Fatima this time, and finally got the name of the Operations Manager. I decided to write to him to give him a chance to put his denial in writing.

A few days after I'd written, I received their "Complaints Procedure Leaflet". They must have had an awful lot of complaints, if they had to organise them. I was given a complaint reference number. Complaints could be made by phone first, it said in the leaflet, or you can write but must "include the nature of the complaint or issue". As if someone would complain without stating what they were complaining about! Anyway, the leaflet came too late for me because I had telephoned, even more than once, and had also written. Quite by chance, I had gone through the right procedure without being told!

There was also a covering letter addressed to me telling me that my letter had been received by the Customer Correspondence Team, although it had been addressed to the Operations Manager who, in the meantime, had changed his title to Operations Director. However, the Operations Director (ex-Operations Manager) did not answer my letter. I'm assuming he exists. It was passed on to the Customer Correspondence Team. The letter was signed by someone else in the absence of one of the people belonging to the Customer Correspondence Team whose first name was Paul. Paul? No, it couldn't be the Paul! The Paul, the needle who disappeared in the CRB haystack when I wanted to speak to him. Was that where he was hiding? In the Customer Correspondence Team? No wonder they couldn't find him. But, now, he'd moved again and wasn't there anymore. He'd disappeared again!

In Bureauland, correspondence has now become a joint venture. Some correspondents will specialise in reading, others in writing, some edit the letters, others fold the letters, a few will stuff envelopes, a couple decide on the postage and, the last link in this great chain of being, licks all the stamps. Even before moving back to England, I had asked CRB to send a form to me in Switzerland. They answered that they couldn't because their computer system didn't have the ability to take foreign addresses. So I gave them the address of my friend in England. CRB sent it to him, and he then forwarded it to me. The person who writes on envelopes in the team, must have been on holiday.

Anyway, in the present CRB saga, I was promised an answer within ten working days, but they transcended the expiry date they had set upon themselves. They are far too harsh on themselves. They did apologise for breaking their own deadline. They proceeded to tell me what I had told them, i.e. they confirmed that they had sent me the form and that they had not received it back for processing. Then they confirmed what I had suspected all along, and I quote: "Whilst I do not doubt that you were not told that a payment would be taken immediately on request, I should explain that telephone Disclosure applications are charged at the point of call". This was followed by heartfelt sorrow on their behalf as they continued "I am sorry to inform you that the money is not refundable". It had obviously pained them somewhat to write that. So much so that they couldn't bring themselves to engage with the other issues I'd brought up in my defence in the letter. Their minds were so overturned that they included other totally irrelevant information. The letter was signed by Paul.

They make their own rules up, break their own rules or adhere to them as it suits depending on which way the wind is blowing. If they say "That's the way it is", it becomes the final judgement. For example, if I were CRB, I could decide that anyone who trod on my foot owed me £29. I would then go around placing my foot under anyone else's who came near me. They don't know that, of course, but I take the money from them and then explain. The government creates these bodies, forgets about them, and subsequently they take on a life of their own. They get bigger and bigger, and more and more powerful, rather like Frankenstein. Unlike Frankenstein though, these entities cannot be banished to the ice mountains.

I could have given up, but I wrote back to them the next day instead. Now that I had found Paul, I wasn't going to let him go. We had been in contact for so long now that I had nearly grown fond of him. I addressed the letter to my Paul and asked him to refer the case to the Chief Executive. That's what they suggested you do in their Complaints Procedure Leaflet, if you weren't happy. And I wasn't exactly ecstatic.

In the letter, I asked them what legal authority they had:
1) to make a charge when no service had been provided
2) to discriminate between those who pay by cheque and card holders.

After about one year's insistence, I took my case to the independent moderator. I got a cheque for £29.-! The moral is: don't give up. Bureaucrats are there to make work for themselves so will thrive in corresponding with you until they have no way out.

20

Another ongoing saga was my endeavour to obtain Qualified Teacher Status (QTS). My friend decided to scour the Internet one evening to find out as much as possible about obtaining English QTS. He came across an interesting piece of information. Switzerland had just adopted the EU directives relating to the mutual recognition of qualifications in the EU. Given that in Switzerland I had taught in the state sector, this was grand news indeed. I decided to apply for recognition in England. Application had to be made to the General Teaching Council for England (GTCE).

How come no-one had told me about this option? Not even the woman on the Teacher Training Agency's stall, at the Roadshow, knew about this. 'Do it yourself' is not the copyright of IKEA. It is also the new way the state treat Jane and Joe Public. Bureaucrats set up mountains of terms, conditions, rules, regulations, knit them together in a rice stitch, one plain and one plural alternated, and then leave it to Jane and Joe Public to unravel it all and make sense out of it. If Jane and Joe get desperate enough, they will go to great lengths to try and make head or tail of the issues to sort them out.

Are bureaucrats out to get on people's nerves on purpose? There might be an element of that. On the whole though, when things go wrong, usually they simply don't know what they are doing. Which brings the GTCE to my mind, via association.

GTCE posted me two sets of forms. Maybe they had a surplus of paper? Each form had been sent on different days and was the mirror-reflection of the other. As I was later to find out, this was an early indication of double trouble. With enthusiasm, my friend and I started to fill the form in straightaway. The sooner we sent it in, the sooner my recognition could be processed. Through no fault of our own because we were careful to fill the forms in exhaustively, tick all the right boxes, quite neatly, and never did ticks trespass over lines. And, we attached all the right bits of paper. Little did we know that seasons would roll over and we'd still be trying to sort QTS out! Only after eighteen months of correspondence, though I had written confirmation from the head of Education in the Italian-speaking Canton, did I come to the conclusion that my cantonal recognition to teach was not the same as the internationally transferable national recognition.

The Blair government has created bureaucratic obscurantism sugared over by superficial spin. That is to say, you will get smiles, politeness and the aura of "we are here to help you", but underneath all that, it is made difficult for the public to actually get what it needs.

Bureaucrats send Jane and Joe Public zigzagging backwards and forwards or, even better, spinning round and round until they're completely confused and exhausted, whether it's from one person to another, one desk to another, one office to another, one building to another, or from one end of town to another. And, quite often without achieving anything whatsoever.

For example, my daughter was looking for a summer job and needed to open a bank account. I thought it was just a case of go in, open the account and walk out again in about fifteen minutes, as you would do in Switzerland. How wrong! An account could not be opened unless we presented two documents of identity with at least one proving her address. My daughter carried her Italian identity card with her at all times. The identity card was fine, but we needed to go home to get her driving licence. We went back to the bank and presented them with what they had requested, the two documents, side-by-side. The young lady disappeared behind the scenes to confer with colleagues to see what reasons they could find to make opening an account impossible and deny the opening of the account altogether. "Sorry, we can't accept this identity card as we are unable to check it". Surely, she must have known that they needed to check the card before we were sent home to get the driving licence?

My daughter had got through immigration with the identity card so why couldn't the bank accept its authenticity on that basis? This might be a naive assumption as if there would be some sort of reciprocal assistance between bureaucrats. These people are so suspicious that I imagine they wouldn't let anyone stand behind them, leave alone venture into a completely unfamiliar territorial field of another bureaucrat. In fact, they seem scared stiff of the likes of themselves. They probably react by becoming meek in each other's respect. It is only where Jane and Joe Public are concerned that they become dogmatic. J&J are made to feel that they might be trying to get away with something. And, anyway, the public get in the way of bureaucrats' already muddled up process.

The bank tried hard to get rid of us, but I insisted. I told them that I was an account holder with them, thinking that they might be softened by an existing customer and appealing to any pity they might harbour within them. I even held out my shiny debit card with their logo on it, and then I handed them my passport. No-can-do. Rather than cause a furore, we left and made our way to another bank. This bank wasn't taking chances either, they wanted to fix an appointment. Opening a bank account, so easy in Switzerland, was something of a rarity, a special occasion in England. My daughter decided to do without!

21

In the meantime, at the adult College where I was teaching Italian, preparations were under way for the imminent inspection. Everyone was chasing around after bits of paper. The amount of paper dished out by management in that period was impressive as was what was written on that very paper. They wrote in such empty high-flown rhetoric. The brainwork that must have gone into it all was not to be underestimated. The paperwork was obviously aimed at subordinates who had lesser brain power than management.

Management assumed that no-one could feel patronised because management was always much more intelligent than subordinates. Given that management pitch the level of intelligence, those subordinates who have a surplus of intelligence need to realise that it will go to waste. Indeed, if you don't suppress your surplus yourself, it will be squashed for you. Smile sweetly, think 'management is great', and you'll be fine. You couldn't make constructive criticism. Improvement was certainly not the priority; the appearance of improvement was. Further along the line, in my experience as a teacher in England, I was to see this mindset again.

One such appearance of improvement took shape in the Quality Assurance Folder. For every course, at this College, you had to have a Quality Assurance Folder. The name itself smacked of improvement and had such an influential ring to it. Teachers had to get the following documents ready for each folder and, it goes without saying, all the work involved was unpaid:

- Scheme of work - a lesson-by-lesson plan for the whole course.

- Lesson plans - one detailed plan for each lesson in which you stated: Tutor name, Course, Date, Time, Health & Safety Considerations, Aims, Learning Outcomes, Equality, Diversity and Differentiation. Then for every activity held within that lesson, you had to write down: Timing, Teaching Point, Teaching Method, Student Activity and Resources. At the end of the lesson, you evaluated each student's progress.

- Induction checklist - a report on initial impressions – this listed seven points about why the class needed an induction. Then we were told about icebreakers, initial assessment activities, Induction to the course (7 headings), ground rules (6 headings), health and safety (6 headings), college facilities in which we were to inform students about the nearest toilet, student noticeboards, learning center (yes, the American spelling - downloaded from the Internet?), Refreshments, Parking/Bike & pram shed (which we didn't have), policy for mobile phones and policy for non-smoking.

- Initial student evaluation forms – in which students were asked if the pace was too fast, if they received homework, how can they be helped to learn more effectively, if delivery was varied, if their individual needs were being met, if resources were suitable, other comments. Students were supposed to know all this at the beginning of the course.

- Progress checklists – 4 sides of boxes to fill

- Individual Learning Plan

- Student assessment and progress checking (checklists, reflective diaries, portfolios)

- Samples of students' work

- Samples of materials used

- End of course student evaluations

- End of course tutor evaluation

- Course report

- Additional Learning Support Form

- Learner Handbook and Folders

- Course Description

Lesson preparation, marking, photocopying, meetings, email correspondence and compiling your own pay sheets were to be added to this workload.

Following a misunderstanding, I was asked to add just one more task to the above. I was ill during the night and this resulted in my not being able to get to my morning lesson which started at 9.30. Some students turned up at the College only to find there was no lesson. This came about because some students set out before 9 o'clock. The office opened at nine. From 8.55 onwards I tried phoning the office at intervals of one minute until someone answered the phone at two minutes past nine. But it was too late. By the time the office workers phoned the students, some had already set out. This happened to two of the students who were furious because they came to College by taxi. The office staff got an earful that morning. I should have informed the students myself, I was told, but the College could not provide me with students' phone numbers or addresses because of the data protection policy. I asked why the office couldn't open at 8.30. "We can't do that, we work 9 to 5".
"Well, why not start courses later then", I suggested.
"We can't do that, courses start at 9.30".

Admin staff were sometimes in the office before nine o'clock but that was kind of hit-n-miss. Even if they were in, they weren't obliged to answer the phone or call anyone until nine o'clock. But teachers were a different species. Outside office hours, teachers themselves had to make calls. Whenever, wherever: teachers always had access to phones. Whether from their home, at the doctor's or even from casualty. Teachers also had to foot the bill for phone calls, too, of course.

Teachers are supposed not to notice that paperwork takes more effort than actually teaching. Although teaching is the only part we are paid for. The idea behind the system is one of financial genius. Cheap and easy. Private commerce could learn a thing or two from the state, if only they'd take notice. Office workers could be asked to go into the office for just one-and-a-half hours a day. They could go and collect their work and take the rest home. That way, you only feel as if you are working for 90 minutes a day because that is the length of time that your presence is required. The rest can be done leisurely at home on your own computer and telephone. Think of the flexibility. You can work whenever and wherever you wish. You wouldn't need to ask for time off for doctor or dentist appointments, picking kids up or any other daytime engagement because you could work in the evenings or at weekends! On a sunny day, you can take your work with you down to the river, sit under a tree and hear the birds chirping while you get on with your work.

The other great advantage is the amount of money employers would save. A great secretary, accountant, etc. could be paid 90 minutes a day pro-rata. The work which goes to make up the rest of the working day would be free of charge to employers. Furthermore, employers must make sure that the employee has a degree, and experience. Moreover, the employers must also ensure themselves that the employee has a post-graduate qualification to practice that profession. Or failing that, the employee is at least in the process of obtaining it. Also, lots of meetings need to be organised, especially in the evenings when everybody's free, to keep an eye on the employees; otherwise, professional standards will decline.

I may have missed the excitement of the OFSTED inspection at the Comprehensive, but I didn't miss its look alike at my College for adults. Preparations were fervent and the mother of all meetings came about shortly before the inspection. We received a letter stating that attendance was obligatory (though unpaid). It was worth giving up one's Friday evening because we were generously repaid with a choice of either tea or granulated coffee and value assorted biscuits nicely laid out on trays. The abundance was such that you could help yourself freely.

I must say that mobilisation had taken place on a grand scale to pass the inspection. This was pass or close. One failure and you're given a second chance. Second failure and you close or change your name. Maybe management didn't want to lose its privilege of playing harmonica with the government's purse strings.

We had been handed detailed sheets quoting the names of all the management staff, their titles, phone numbers and email addresses. All bound in an expensive ring-binder with dynamic modern geometric coloured patterns on the cover. As a burden, and the lowest order in the grand scheme of things, teachers were not mentioned. Teachers would have a better life next time around, as far as can be reasonably expected. To get rid of teachers entirely would have been the best solution, then even more money would circulate in management: the most important aspect in education, as they were the constant breeders of good ideas. However, teachers were given a mention in the organigram. Justly placed at the bottom, on a par with the caretakers.

As it was, teachers had to be kept on the books in order to undergo inspection. Inspectors wanted to sit in lessons which had teachers in them. Teachers were warned that even walls had ears when inspectors were around. There was no such thing as telling someone something in confidence. It would backfire like divine retribution on all of us. We would be left without jobs.

Given that my lessons were first thing on a Monday morning, I was told my lesson would not be inspected because the inspectors had meetings with the management upon arrival. So, I started my lesson in the certainty that big brother would leave us in peace. Twenty minutes into the lesson, the head of Languages, even smiling at me, obligingly opened the door and introduced me to the inspector. I was expecting the inspector to have two heads, but was quite taken aback to find she was a normal human being like the rest of us. In fact, she even looked nice, smiling and friendly. I wasn't going to let them intimidate me. I was being paid a pittance. They had the best deal. And, I wouldn't miss reading all the emails I received, on a quasi daily basis, from management keeping me up to date on every insignificant minute detail.

I picked up my lesson plan and another form, which I'd been given by the College, and placed the sheets of paper on a desk towards the back of the classroom. My students were sitting in a circle in the middle and I with them. That way the line of sight between the inspector and me was obscured by the head of one of my students. So, I could continue the lesson as if there were no observer. We carried on as usual, talking, reading, writing difficult words on the board and generally enjoying ourselves and having a good laugh, until it was time for the break. I went to get a coffee while the inspector talked to the students. To my disappointment, the inspector decided to stay for more, until the end, in fact. I did some listening and writing practice because I thought the inspector would like all five skills (reading, listening, writing, speaking and grammar) covered in the span of a lesson.

The lesson came to an end and the inspector beckoned me to her. Apart from the fact that I had an appointment with my physiotherapist, I had nothing else to do. It is assumed that teachers will give up their free time upon demand. I told her it would have to be quick. She looked quite startled. She said that my lesson was relaxed, varied, instructive and good fun. She enjoyed it very much. I had covered all the abilities, too. She knew a little Italian herself and wished she could join the course. Going to the meat of the argument, I asked what mark she was going to give me. She replied that she could not tell me, but that I should be able to hazard a good guess from her comments. She had nothing negative to say, only compliments, so it must have been really high. "I really must go now!", I exclaimed. As I was moving towards the door to leave, she called me back and handed me one of the sheets of paper I had given to her at the beginning of the lesson. "I think this was meant for you", she said. "What is it?" "It's a form asking for feedback on the inspection". Was it possible that I was inspecting the inspector? I hurriedly shoved it in my bag. I believe it's still there.

Now, if a teacher receives excellent feedback after a lesson from an official observer (that the management are scared to shivers by) why does she have to be patronised to humiliation, on cold dark winter evenings, by pseudo-intellectual teacher trainers?

Management lived in the inspection's afterglow for weeks. Re-inspection had been passed and the euphoria resulted in even more trees being slaughtered. In one Newsletter, staff were informed about the setting up of an ILEG, the modularisation of "L" courses, the re-launch of BSL courses, of the GOLF scheme, of the ILT Strategy and that after the LLB had left, the PIAP would start. Details were also given about LS and ALS as well as SROCN and OCN accreditation AKA "F" courses. There was also a large section headed 'Tutors come, tutors go...'.

Their sentences were brilliantly structured. They had to be because the writing came from those people who were also developing teacher training and giving advice on how our essays should be written so as to achieve our qualification in teaching adults. I quote one sentence as an example:

"A student's situation may change once the course have begun and may need to reassess their needs..." This is an extremely sophisticated criss-cross accordance between verbs and nouns/pronouns. A lot of the courses rotated around Basic Skills in English, maybe Management should have joined as students.

With the advent of the new academic year, I was offered an 'F' course. This was new to me, so before accepting, I needed to know what it entailed exactly. I didn't want to get into any F courses that would take up all my waking hours. In the Newsletter, there was some information about these F courses, which I started reading with great interest.

F courses were extremely important for funding, it turned out. It was essential that these courses lasted 30 weeks because a course lasting 29 weeks would loose (sic!) the College £960 for a class of twelve participants. For these courses Accreditation Folders were essential and detailed instructions on how to run the scheme were in a folder especially put together for the occasion. There were also lots of meetings to attend. I'm afraid I must have a low attention span and got sleepy just reading about it all. Much more work had been created around these courses than non-accredited courses, it seemed to me. No talk of extra money for the workload. I sent an email stating that I could take on the teaching but no paperwork. That was the equivalent of saying that I could not take the course on. They could offer their F course to someone even more desperate than me.

22

During my time at the College for adults, I was suffering from a medical condition. I must have looked worse than I thought. A teacher said she thought she felt rotten until she saw me paley loitering. The symptoms pointed to the possibility of cancer. My GP tried to get me an urgent appointment with a consultant at the local hospital. Readers who have been through a similar experience know how nerve-wracking the wait can be. After asking around, I found out that it was normal procedure to wait weeks, even months, for appointments with consultants. I couldn't believe the resignation of the English.

It was on a Thursday, when I decided to take action. I sensed it would be no good waiting around. I was so frustrated and angry that I decided to phone my doctor in Switzerland. He gave me the telephone number of a consultant who would be able to help me. I telephoned and the receptionist asked me to ring back after a couple of hours as she had fixed a telephone consultation with the consultant for me. I phoned back at the prescribed time and, in the meantime, the consultant had looked up my medical history. The consultant said I should be seen straightaway. Given that I couldn't get there for the next day, a Friday, she could see me first thing Monday morning. I flew to Switzerland over the weekend and was seen at 8 a.m. on Monday.

The doctor was furious with the English system for putting me through so much anguish. The consultant confirmed I didn't have any dangerous illnesses. She also took me off the medication I'd been prescribed by my GP in England and put me on other tablets.

I told a Swiss friend of mine about the long time you often have to wait to see a consultant in England. I also told her that even cancer patients often have to wait for radiotherapy. Referring to the medical services and the government, she exclaimed: "Aren't they ashamed of themselves?"

So, I went back to England. When I came out of customs, I rushed to catch my train as it was due to leave in five minutes. When I arrived at the station, I discovered that trains were cancelled. I had never heard of trains being cancelled before. Trains had been replaced by a bus service. I told the man on duty that I could never make it down to the buses in the few minutes left as I didn't even know where the bus station was. Indifference. Had I been in his place, I would have contacted the driver and asked him to wait. Surely he could see how pale I was. But he was not ready to put himself out.

As it was, I was just in time to get down to the buses to see my bus whizz past me. I waved to the driver, but he didn't stop. A minimum amount of logic told me that buses should have left about ten minutes after the train's expected departure time, to allow anyone, who went to the station first, time enough to get from the train station to the bus station. So I sat on my case, and waited an hour for the next bus, which was late.

It was weeks before I obtained an appointment with a consultant in England. My condition had cleared up completely by then. And, I knew it wasn't some terrible disease.

23

I was still job hunting for a full-time post. I decided to try applying only for good teaching jobs. So I tried independent schools and a few sixth-form colleges. I made up my mind not to complete any application forms at all. I would only send my CV and a covering letter. I wanted to be considered on my academic strength and not on my form-filling ability. If the school couldn't be bothered to accept my application as it was, then the place wasn't for me.

A few schools sent me forms in reply to my application. It pained me to consign them to the bin, what a waste of paper. One sixth-form college was a bureaucratic masterpiece. The College carried the name of a famous artist. After living his life surrounded by beauty, I imagine he would have been absolutely furious to know how his name had been taken in vain by churners out of gibberish. They sent me thirty-three sides of printed sheets of paper. Of course, they also sent a copious form. Not only. But also, they sent three different sets of instructions on how to complete it. English teachers were not what they used to be and had to be guided step by step. As for filling forms in, who better to provide instructions than the minds that had created those very forms?

The sets of instructions were headed:
Set 1: "How to Fill Out Application Form"
Set 2: "Help with completing your form"
Set 3: "Important Note for Completion of the Application Form"

Prospective English teachers needed to be told that they should "Try to address each of the criteria using words such as 'I plan' or 'I organise'." These academics, qualified with their formidable learning, towered above any teacher of English, in a great many aspects including that of précis writing. How such bright sparks all congregated at this very College was indeed a reason for wonder. They shared their assistance with great generosity. Anyone appointed to attend an interview with their recruiting staff must consider themselves truly honoured to have the opportunity of being in the company of such endowed humans. The outcome of such an assembly would have to be placed much lower than the honour thirty minutes in their distinguished company would bestow.

Some might think that they, too, traded clarity for pomposity. It is, however, true that this College proclaimed in one place what it denied in another. This incongruity must have slipped by them, somehow. On Set 1 of their instructions, they stated that "Curriculum Vitae will not be accepted. You must fill out an application form addressing all criteria". This was all written in capitals and in bold and, as if that were not enough, they underlined the "not" and "all", for good measure. It is best not to take any chances with thick English teachers who cannot pick up nuances. Then on Set 2, they more compliantly stated that "CVs will be accepted but must cover all the selection criteria listed for this job". I was somewhat confused about whether or not they accepted CVs without application forms. I suppose that they must have done given that elsewhere they had written that "the best people are appointed to deliver our services" and that they "will only consider applicants for jobs on the basis of their relevant experience, qualifications, skills and abilities". Was it only the best or only the desperate who filled in their application forms, read all their documentation and complied?

Their foresight led them to know that I was going to write to them. The date on their covering letter was that of a week before I had even asked for information about the job. How did they do it? Admittedly, they had not been able to guess my name so addressed it to an anonymous "Dear Applicant". Like so many similar organisations, they carried 'investors in people' status. It is clear that they had a huge interest in people.

Out of the thirty-three sheets, one was headed "Selection Criteria". On this page, the expression "Selection Criteria" was repeated fifteen times. This was to hammer the term home to candidates who were not quite as bright as the writers were. That they got their "criterion" and "criteria" mixed up must have been due to some external force. They were also extremely careful to "give employees clear information about selection and training". The sheer fun of it. They had a "school improvement team" which made one wonder what they needed that for.

In Switzerland, we were told that three aspects make a good teacher:
1) excellent knowledge of one's subject
2) the ability to convey that knowledge
3) being able to empathise with students

I think that the above points were embedded somewhere in the thirty-three pages of the documentation sent to me by this College. It's just that they extended the points, and added so much, that you couldn't see them anymore. They added, added, and added wonderfully constructed rules, regulations, requirements, instructions, imperatives, orders, obligations, enforcements, conditions, commands, directions, standards, measures, codes, facts, figures, theories, ideas, explanations, speculations, specifications, suggestions, descriptions, representations, statements, views, opinions, beliefs, thoughts, meditations, principles, concepts, intentions, purposes, procedures, headings, sub-headings, lines, paragraphs, and columns. Fruit of work spanning over quite a long period of time and extracted from a wide spectrum of sources, I dare say. And, all stipulated in repeated sequences of such long, flowing and meandering prose and with such proper authority and circumstance. I really do wonder how they managed to fit it all on just thirty-three pages. It is a question of synthesizing ability. And, it makes such a great long-lasting impression on the recipients as they are supplied with over a year's stock of paper for shopping lists.

The grand finale was a wacky "If you think you like the sound of us please come and join our team!"

24

Another College got their sheets in a twist. Along with their application form, and the many accompanying printed sheets of paper, they quite accidentally included a set of instructions entitled "Instructions to College Staff". These were detailed step-by-step instructions for the immense task awaiting the form administrators as set out by the POM (Procedure Office Manager).

It emerged that POM-POMs closely invigilated on the form administrators and instructed them in writing as to which forms were needed, what to do with the forms, which forms to remove, how to check the forms, how to put the sheets together, how to store them, how to identify the slips of the short-listed candidates, how to tick the 'short-listed' box, how to identify the monitoring slip and tick the 'appointed' box, how to staple, or fasten together, the monitoring slips of all the candidates who applied for the post, and what to do to the top form. Which was, first and foremost, to place the form at the top of the pile. And then to:
1) tick the full-time box as appropriate;
2) enter the grade at which the appointment was made;
and finally
3) enter the closing date for the vacancy.

Being a POM-POM is terribly hard graft because you have to identify all the crucial stages in dealing with applications with great care, attention and patience. The manner of treating the forms and the action taken thereafter cannot proceed in the customary way of letting the form administrators deal with the situation as they see fit. Precise rules must be laid down, firmly and clearly, otherwise someone, somewhere in the office, might use initiative.

25

I went for an interview for a job with another sixth-form college, one that accepted a CV. I must admit, I was pleasantly surprised with what I found. This was a private college. They were taking students who the comprehensive system had failed. They were doing a grand job because these students were getting GCSEs and A levels denied to them by state education. In other words, in the mayhem of state comprehensives, these students had achieved next to nothing. But, many of these students had gone on to become dentists and doctors. If it hadn't been for this College, they would probably be spending the rest of their lives believing themselves second-rate citizens. From being part of a sub-culture, they were entering society at the height of their potential. Because most of the students were second generation immigrants, they excelled in science subjects rather than humanities. English was a difficult subject for them because most spoke another language at home.

The way good results were obtained here was no secret. Very easy, in fact. The teachers stood in the front of the class, explained their subject to the students, told the students what to do, and they did it. Each lesson was extended by homework. Then heads down and get on with it. No sign of forms anywhere. Talk and chalk, focused and efficient. In other words, the fancy frills of state embroidery were left undone.

Expectations from students were high both at the College and at home. Those expectations could only be met through hard work. And the students delivered what was expected. I still remember Mr Morris, a school-teacher of mine, telling our class that good results could only be obtained in one of two ways. The first was to work hard, while the second was to be a genius. He added that he had never met a genius.

26

I obtained interviews with a few independent schools that accepted my CV. All of them paid my travel expenses and offered me lunch. You were treated like a guest.

One was a religious foundation. It was set in the most beautiful grounds. The place pulsed with money; it was everywhere. They had their own impressive chapel and a sports centre that many towns would have been envious of: swimming-pool, tennis courts and even beautiful inexpensive accommodation for teachers. As much as I've grown fond of pupils in the past, it has never been enough to want to spend twenty-four hours with them.

I'd looked at their results on the Internet and discovered that their English results were not as good as for the other subjects. It is curious, this is not the first time that I have found this to be the case in schools. At the interview, I wanted to find out what was the cause of this outcome. I suspected it was linked to the fact that religion gave you a slant on the world which narrowed it down. I could only teach at 360 degrees.

Free or critical thinking and religion are at antipodes. If these parents had sent their children to this School, probably it was because they wanted their children to follow beliefs. This brings with it the consequence of not embarking into too much critical thinking. Already, during my trial lesson, I was worried that I would touch on some taboo subject. Why I ever applied for the job, I don't know. The manacles forged by religion on these minds tightened around my stomach.

The head of English had recently left and a new one had been appointed. Given that the new head of English would start in September, one of the English teachers was appointed acting head of department. I asked her why she thought the English results lagged behind the rest. She denied this was so and asked where I had obtained that information from. "From the statistics posted on the Internet", I answered. "No, it's not true", she denied again. The first step towards tackling a problem is admitting you have one. Then I tried the same observation on the headteacher. She said that students do learn to respect other points of view. 'Well, that's all we need', I thought, 'a school which doesn't teach respect for other people's views! Whatever next?' However, respecting other people's points of view and placing in doubt your own, in order to acquire a broader view, is totally different.

There was something odd in the English department. It seemed that three teachers out of the four in the department were leaving. Apart from the head of department, two English teachers were about to leave and be replaced. I spoke to one of them over lunch. She neither praised nor criticised the school, except to say that the food was delicious. I had already decided I didn't want to work there and didn't want to get into long discussions.

After lunch I was interviewed by the headteacher. With serious concern for what I might be hiding, she quizzed me about my not allowing them to take up pre-interview references. "Every other teacher has allowed us to contact a previous employer!" My ex-Swiss employers were getting fed up with incessant requests for references for every potential interview. After a senior education manager had remarked to me "Are the people in management in English schools stupid, or do they pretend to be stupid?", I insisted that schools could only take up references when they made me a job offer. After all, CRB establish you are not a danger to kids, GTCE recognises your qualifications, your degree shows your academic qualifications, a trial lesson confirms you can teach and if the school likes you, and you like the school, references can be taken up when all this is settled.

Anyway, I didn't like the school. The next day I sent the headteacher an email saying that I no longer wished to be considered. Also, because I had found something rather special. I had an interview with an excellent independent school!

27

A breath of fresh air. An independent girls' school with no religious connections. I saw the headteacher first. A tip-top lady, warm, friendly and professional. She told me that the salary offered was at the top of the scale. Sixty percent more than the salary paid to me at the Comprehensive. However, I would have to obtain Qualified Teacher Status because it was a requirement of theirs. She assured me they would put me on the course, if I were appointed. I did explain to her my ongoing travails with the General Teaching Council. I asked for what reason the teacher I was replacing was leaving. I was told that she was retiring. I also found out that the head of English had taught at the school for seventeen years, been head of English for three years, but was now leaving.

The headteacher thought that having had experience teaching in Switzerland could only be positive given that its education system had an excellent reputation. "Indeed it has", I confirmed. "My two children both obtained their university entrance qualifications at our local state school in Switzerland. They both learnt to speak and write four languages. My daughter took the Classics option, so added Ancient Greek and Latin to her curriculum, whilst my son concentrated more on Sciences. They are both at university now. One in Florence and the other in Zurich".

Yes, I had been spoilt in Switzerland. The fact that I had experienced what practising one's profession in a serious way meant, contributed to my frustration in sub-standard institutions. At the same time, having the Swiss positive experience behind me meant I knew the rewards teaching can bring. Had I started my teaching career in English comprehensives straight out of university, like so many others, I would have changed profession. I knew there had to be better in England. And, this looked like being much better.

I was given a guided tour of the school by a senior teacher. A walking interview. The school had undergone a lot of renovation and the results were impressive. We walked through the grounds and entered the school through the library. Ceiling-high shelves packed with old and new volumes, sprawlings of flowers, and silence. A large portrait of an illustrious lady hung on the wall and looked onto readers like a patron saint. No doubt, she had contributed a great deal to the school and to girls' education as a whole. Some girls sat quietly reading at an antique polished table and didn't notice us. Culture and a hunger to feed the intellect can never be obsolete. Noise here would have been heresy, you could hear a pin drop. Difficult to just walk through, though. The atmosphere enticed you to remove a book from one of the shelves and join the readers. The librarian sat at a semi-circle desk from where she had an excellent overall view of the whole library. She smiled as we passed. Contrastingly, the other half of the library was dynamic. A long row of computers at which girls sat researching, typing and exchanging information on this and that.

This was a happy place. Some girls turned and smiled, others were busily looking for books, while others were coming and going. We left the library and walked across the grounds again to another wing of the school. We passed a large pond on our right and a statue of a girl reading on our left. We went past the swimming pool and up the stairs to the classroom where my trial lesson would take place.

I had been asked to discuss language and content in a poem of my choice. The head of English observed the lesson. We had got there a few minutes before the lesson was due to begin. The sun was teeming in, so I pulled the vertical blinds across the windows and pulled the string which turned the blades and closed out the heat. The girls soon poured into the classroom. Two girls saw I was having difficulties with the video and inquired if they could help. They took care of that task, while I concentrated on getting the over-head projector in the right position. I placed my transparencies in the correct order. All systems go, I was soon ready to start.

After introducing myself, to break the ice, I projected a picture supposed to be me as an Italian baby covered in spaghetti. The girls giggled and a few suspected it wasn't me at all. The aim had been reached, it intrigued them and made them sit up wondering what else I'd have up my sleeve. The girls here were so sparky, alive and bright.

I gave them all a copy of "Funeral Blues" by W. H. Auden. I had left the last word of every other line out and asked them to guess it. The missing words needed to rhyme with the word in the last line above it. It also needed to make sense with the line it was in. We did the first one together. What rhymed with 'phone' and kept a dog quiet? That was an easy one. It got them working knowing that they could tackle the rest. When they had finished I played the excerpt from "Four Weddings and a Funeral", in which the poem is majestically recited, so that they could check their answers. This also gave them a feeling for the poem. I then projected a completed version of the poem, so the girls could check their answers in case they hadn't caught a word or two. It is important that no-one is left behind.

To give them a sense of images created in our minds by poetry, I had brought pictures of everything I could find which was mentioned in the poem. Phones, dogs, bones, policemen, gloves, aeroplanes, doves, bows, etc. I left the natural elements until last: the sun, the moon, ocean and woods. And, lastly I projected a blank rectangle and asked them what it was. They came up with some very intelligent answers. Yes, it could symbolise nothing, silence, death - uncluttering the world of everything. These bright girls fired my enthusiasm. They lapped it up. The exchanges went on until the end of the lesson. I let the discussion take the course of their sparky contributions, while slipping in the important points I had intended to discuss. The discussion went in crescendo until we reached the apex and conclusion. The girls burst out into applause. I was overcome by a wave of emotion, and tears welled up. I knew I had got the job!

It is still possible to infuse children with love of Literature; to motivate them to read more. The government has taken the joy out of teaching. Running after grades has impoverished education. The biggest mistake that state education is making is that it reflects society. Copying society by offering children easy answers like banks offer adults easy money. Education should offer a different outlook on society. Education should maintain high standards and not bend over backwards to award nearly everyone sub-standard qualifications. The Blair government has turned education into Alice's Wonderland in which almost everyone has to win and almost everyone has to have prizes. It has not worked. In fact, it has backfired.

The BBC reported that figures released on 22nd September 2005 by the Higher Education Statistics Agency showed that top universities in the UK were rejecting more students from state schools in favour of rivals from the fee-paying sector. On 20th September 2005, The Times published an article in which the headteacher of an independent school branded the Education Secretary, Ruth Kelly, as a "disaster". He stated "Frankly I don't care how many politicians say something to the contrary. Rigour has gone out of the window. Results are massaged so that they appear better than they are".

The way high grades are obtained is easy. Assessment Objectives are set out by examination boards and teachers drill pupils to hit those objectives. Therefore, assembly line teaching ensues. Paradoxically, even creative writing is drilled! And, if students are also drilled in fringe subjects, forcing total school statistics up comes even easier. Even so, statistics still have to be manipulated to look good. Unpublished results obtained by the BBC, show that one in six schools, whose results apparently have improved since 2001, actually became worse at English and maths. That included some of the schools listed as "the most improved". The Times reported that "spin does not do justice to the extraordinary manner in which the Department for Education and Skills has rewritten its figures on university admissions. Apparently following the maxim that if you are going to fib, fib big".

Anyway, the head of English then led me to her office to interview me. She asked about my teaching techniques and they seemed to be perfectly in tune with hers. So as to boost my ratings, I told her I was going to write a book about my experience of returning to England after living abroad for many years. "Don't forget to mention education!", she exclaimed. Confident that my days in bedlam were over, I hadn't the slightest inkling that yet more material for my book was still to be delivered in spades.

28

September soon came around again and I started at the school. I had received no induction either from the old or new head of English. I had e-mailed the old head of English during the summer to find out what exam boards and subject options they followed and then downloaded the syllabuses from the Internet.

Confusion seemed to be the name of the game. Little was I to know that the meddling and muddling spin of the state was to appear at this school in the form of Alastair Campbell in a skirt: the new head of English. The previous friendly and open-minded head of English was replaced by a deputy-head of English from a large Comprehensive. Let's call her Rhonda. On the whole, our department was not a happy one. We had a staffroom divided into groups of desks, each group a department. The English area was in the far corner and maths was next to English. For the first time in my life, I wished I had taken a degree in maths because I envied the banter and laughter which came from that area. The head of maths was certainly dextrous in creating team spirit. But, I did have two delightful colleagues in my department, a young woman, who also taught Latin, who I'll call Octavia, and an older teacher who was one of the gentlest and one of the most enlightened women I had ever come across. I will call her

Rose. There were five of us altogether. The other English teacher was also head of year, I'll call her Dawn.

Rose, Octavia and I were put under pressure by Rhonda. Perhaps because she was an existing member of the school management team, Dawn was left alone. Weaknesses were looked for. For example, Rhonda soon noticed that Rose was not dextrous with computers so started to taunt her about not being able to use the newly installed whiteboards. Rose had a long and distinguished career behind her. It was the policy of the school for new teachers to observe a lesson of every member of their own department's lessons. To hear Rose talk about Literature and recite poetry was magic. Notwithstanding her unfamiliarity with digital pens, Rose got her son into the English faculty at Oxford! I did not get the same rush of enthusiasm when I sat in the other lessons.

Every day became a test. Rhonda came up with the idea of organising the departmental Christmas lunch on my only day off. Even though I had had thirty-five teachers under me in Switzerland, I would never have organised a social event and left someone out. I had the weakness of vagueness and unwillingness to see Literature through her government imposed view. That was my 'fault'. It needed correction.

What surprised me most about teaching Literature to pupils in exam classes was how they were not used to coming up with their own interpretation. These pupils could not accept nuances and thought that there could only be one right answer. This was a real eye-opener. I couldn't believe it. If Keats' "Grecian Urn" had only one single interpretation, then his Ode would have been relegated to some dusty archive and forgotten by now. Once we have understood a piece of Literature, we can put it away and forget about it. But this cannot happen to great Literature because its infinite variety of multiple interpretations will always keep it alive - that is the very reason why it is great. Because I accepted any plausible interpretation of a poem, I

104

was accused of being vague. Poems convey ideas which are necessarily not clear and not totally comprehensible. There cannot be one right answer. I would give the pupils my interpretation and accept theirs, too. But they saw this as being contradictory. They could not accept ambiguity. It is this very impossibility of reaching a complete understanding of a poem which gives us the flutters when we see a new meaning in it. Great Literature does not want to be completely understood - it wants to be seen as rich and complex. It is about leaving the concrete and entering the unlimited intangible world.

There is no time for the unlimited when teaching exam classes. It all has to be clear-cut, harnessed and put into little boxes. That's why it is impossible to convey what Literature really is. My vagueness was fast becoming famous. One day the headteacher sat in my class. When revising a poem, I gave my interpretation of an image, some pupils didn't agree. In fact, they had seen a video the year before, which gave another interpretation. Therefore, both the pupils and the headteacher saw me as incompetent because I had not given the same interpretation as the video, so I could not possibly be right. The headteacher thought it a good idea for me to look for that video, so that I could find out what the prescribed interpretation was.

There's something very wrong in letting pupils believe that Literature is one-dimensional. It's a kind of fraud to give students a qualification in Literature without their knowing its purpose. We lead our pupils to believe that they know what it's about when they don't. The sore truth is that understanding what Literature is about has become superfluous because it is not necessary given that you can pass your exams anyway by drilling students to feed examiners their Assessment Objectives. Hit those on the head and you get high marks. Drilling is the exact opposite of the independent thinking needed for interpretation and appreciation. If I cannot convey the joy and passion I have for my subject, then what is the point of teaching it? Do I dwindle my passion down into one-dimensional soundbites?

Do I turn what is beautifully complex to trite? I suppose I might be seen as a great innocent. I thought that what mattered to me would matter to others. Seeing my wonderful subject as merely a means to 'another good grade' saddened me and took the joy out of teaching.

I was shocked and angered that Literature had become purely materialistic. I believe an analogy can be made by looking at the difference between love and prostitution. Something highly beautiful has been turned into a utilitarian business deal. You give me the bits of information I demand, and I'll give you your qualification - mechanical exchange - cold calculation.

One Year 11 mother came down to the school to complain about my vagueness. Added to that, I had also shown the girls a teacher's pack, information for teachers, which I was passing straight on to the girls, this mother claimed. In fact, it came from resources for teachers to use with pupils in class. Because it had "teachit" written at the bottom, the girl assumed it was for teachers. Why I wasn't called to the meeting, so that I could explain, I don't know. Episodes directly regarding you were reported. You could defend yourself at a distance. When information is passed from one person to another, it can become distorted. When managing in Switzerland, if there was any question regarding a teacher, the first thing I did was to say, diplomatically of course, that we had every confidence in our teacher and then invite that teacher to take part in the discussion in order to get everything out into the open and let the teacher explain. As it was, the deputy-head saw the mother, the girl was called out of my lesson, and then Rhonda got a look-in, too. I really did not like, and was not used to, having all this talking about people behind their backs. The whole issue took on such gravity. I was then called to the deputy-head's office and told about the meeting.

She spoke to me as if I had committed a crime. I was quizzed about my vagueness and resources. I explained that the resources were meant for use in class and gave her copies to prove this. In fact, I had found these resources on my own. If I had been handed a detailed scheme of work, all this would not have happened. I had to go hunting round for material, it was all over the place so lesson preparation took me hours. I had no previous material from the system in England to draw on. The next query was about my vagueness. I got so fed up with the criticism and scant support that I told her that I was ready to chuck the job in. She said that if I left, they would give me a good reference. I should have given my notice in, rather than put myself through more of this treatment. Unfortunately, I got it wrong and stayed. The deputy-head decided to come and sit in my class, so that she could give the mother some feedback. No way this would have happened in Switzerland.

Once again, we were discussing a poem. Instead of saying that metaphors, images, etc. could mean this and that, I gave just one interpretation. I had to get into a 'one interpretation mode'. But, I couldn't get anything right because everyone knew more than me about Literature. In the poem, a jeep was described as if it were a man-eating monster. I explained this was personification. Some girls contradicted me saying it wasn't personification. The deputy-head had a grievance about that, too. "It is not personification, they are right because the jeep was not described as if it were a person. That's why it's called **person**ification, it's got to be a person", she told me. As if I didn't have enough to do, after the lesson, I hunted around for material to prove my point. I found the definition in Abrams' Dictionary of Literary Terms. It proved that: personification is the animation of inanimate objects. I photocopied it and put it in her pigeon hole. And when, during her observation, I wrote the word diction on the board, telling them it meant choice of words, some girls reached for a dictionary because they didn't believe me. "Semantics" seemed to mean "choice of words" here. I brought this up with Dawn in the staffroom. No, they'd always used "semantics", she told me with impressive confidence.

During our meeting, the deputy-head had also told me that the pupils only got one chance in life, and it was not to be squandered. Did she mean I was squandering that chance?

The vagueness issue had also made its way up to my Year 12 class which I shared with Rhonda. I was teaching them Blake for the poetry section of their AS and Rhonda was teaching them <u>Wuthering Heights</u> for the novel section. Therefore, the pupils had a direct comparison between my views of Literature and hers. We had looked at Blake's symbolism. I explained that symbolism could not be categorically defined with one interpretation. For example, Blake's lamb could symbolise Jesus, innocence, gentleness, nature ... all four, and even more. They told Rhonda that I didn't know what Blake's symbols stood for. Rhonda picked me up on this saying that I needed to be less vague. When we came to Blake's Rose, I started off with one interpretation: the sexual one. They wanted to know how I was sure that Blake meant that, as they thought it rather far-fetched: Blake could not have such a dirty mind. I told them I wasn't sure he might have meant just that and proceeded to give them about another ten interpretations - they asked for it! Anyway, when the exam results came through they did better in Blake than in <u>Wuthering Heights</u>.

Preparation for Year 11 mock exams was underway. For the four-way poetry comparison, I wanted to teach nearly all the poems, but Rhonda said that only a few would do. The pupils started complaining that they might not have enough poems to choose from, if they got an unfamilar theme to discuss in the exam. So they went to complain to Rhonda. Then when I started to revise poems from different cultures, Rhonda told me not to revise them and to switch to Media straightaway. When the pupils complained that they effectively needed practice on these poems, she said I should be teaching these poems and not be doing Media. So I switched back to the poems ... The pupils saw this as to mean that I did not know what I was doing. They were right. I was totally confused. This pattern of muddling and meddling repeated itself day after day even in the most banal tasks like organising a theatre trip for my AS class leading me to book, cancel and book again.

As it turned out, my mock results were the best. The next time around Rose's were the best, but she was accused of having told the pupils the questions beforehand. Something she would never do. What was the point anyway? Rhonda should have been happy that she had such a wonderful teacher in the department. There was no winning. If you were good, you had to be dishonest. If you were no good, well, you were simply no good. In order to be really good, you had to be part of management.

My Year 8 had written the most fantastic parodies of some Shakespeare sonnets. They also decorated them beautifully, and we created two anthologies, which I told them to treasure for the rest of their lives. With the help of two girls, we pinned some up for display on the walls of the classroom for parents' evening. Of course, we also placed their class number at the top of their display. They were proud of their work. When Rhonda saw the display, she said it should be changed to look better. She would do that. To my dismay, whilst fiddling around with the display she removed the letter which defined which class in Year 8 had written the poems. It could have been any teacher's.

So, because of our supposed inadequacies, we English teachers had to have individual weekly meetings with Rhonda, as well as the departmental meetings. This was seen as getting the department on the right track given that we were going all over the place. After the meetings, she would write up the Minutes. I asked if I could have detailed schemes of work, so I would know exactly what I should be doing. I got one-and-a-half typewritten pages explaining, that although there were no comprehensive schemes of work, I had all sorts of things instead: weekly meetings with her, an external course, past papers and mark schemes, where resources were, teacher's guides, etc. In order to tell my side of meetings, I had to write up my comments about the Minutes! This added to my already heavy workload. And to cap it all, new-staff induction meetings were on my day off. I made the effort of attending because I was floundering and needed to know how the system worked. After a few weeks the deputy-head teacher told me not to attend any more of these induction meetings. What made my job harder still was that English teachers were expected to cover double subject GCSE (Language and Literature) in little more class time than some single subjects were allowed.

It was during one of the weekly putting-Anna-on-the-right-track meetings that Rhonda laid her eyes on my Year 10. Classwork was proceeding swimmingly. Something had to spoil it. When Rhonda realised that I had the intention of working my way through the whole of Twelfth Night, she looked at me as if I were a little green woman from outer space. She told me to concentrate on key passages and video the rest. So against my will, I started to do as I was told. Rose, the other green woman, who had so far got away with it, was going through the whole play with another class. Some girls came into lesson one morning complaining that Rose's class was going through the whole play and they felt short-changed. It seemed to them that having excerpts videoed was not serious teaching. I agreed with them. I wanted to teach them properly, but I told them that I had had orders to skip sections.

What seemed like an ideal job was disintegrating from day to day. After management had seen my Year 10 coursework results for Twelfth Night, out of 21 students one girl got a B, the others all obtained A* or A grades, the deputy head and the headteacher's attitude towards me changed. But it was too late, I had already decided to go. I was not staying for more of that treatment. It was revolving doors in the English department. Apart from Rhonda and Dawn, we all started looking for jobs elsewhere. Four separate advertisements appeared in the TES for English teachers at the school in little more than a year.

I left without having a job to go to. I found some temporary work at a school in Switzerland that I had worked for in the past. In their summer Newsletter, Management spun that I had left to go back to Switzerland for family reasons. I left because I was totally frustrated with the way the school treated Literature, and us poor English teachers.

29

But, I was soon back in England!

One morning, I received a letter from the Department for Education and Skills. In truth, I had forgotten about them, but their letter brought it all back to me again.

Looking at their headed paper, I wondered if they had been evicted and their phones cut off. The reason for this was the absence of contact details on their headed paper. Very worrying. Sans address, sans phone number, sans everything except "department for education and skills" followed by the modern instances of "creating opportunity, releasing potential, achieving excellence" – maybe they should try moving towards their latter aim by putting capital letters where they are needed. They were, indeed, playing many parts. With or without premises.

The reason for leaving their details out could have been due to absent-mindedness. After all, creating opportunity, releasing potential and achieving excellence, all in one go, took up a lot of mental space. They probably didn't have any left over to remember to include their details. Or, as I suspect, was more likely, they left the details out on purpose because they do not want to be disturbed. By now, I had seen too much of bureaucracy to think that much good could come from that direction.

The letter requested that I took part in some market research. To improve service to customers, you know. They wanted my opinion on the quality of their replies to customer's letters and emails given that I had written to them at one stage. But why do they call members of the public "customers"? What is being bought and sold? We are their employers, surely. Through our taxes we pay their salaries. I suppose if we want to look at this as a commercial transaction, we are paying them to render a good service and create opportunity, release potential and achieve excellence. They need a lot of tax payers' money for such grand schemes.

As I was saying, I originally came into contact with this laudable entity on the rebound, shortly after contacting the GTCE. I sought to get recognition of my qualification as a teacher of adults. I looked for the Department of Education and Skills' details over the web and found their email address. Unfortunately, the email bounced back because the email address posted on the site was wrong. Maybe they had released all their potential and had run out. If they had had a little left over, they could have posted the correct address. However, I'm sure they'll soon accumulate more potential and start releasing it again into the atmosphere to achieve excellence.

Anyway, I wrote to them and, damn my giddy aunt, they called me within a matter of days. Not only, the man on the other end of the line was helpful and full of common sense. It is true that, like the rest of them, he was sorry that my qualification couldn't be recognised because I was a British citizen. Had I been of any other nationality, I would have been recognised. But as it was being British turned sour on me. It wasn't a question of ability, only of nationality, so I was not to take offence.

However, he did understand my predicament. I told him about my odyssey through the state education system and with the GTCE. He had a Jekyll and Hyde approach. When he was understanding or said something sensible, he stressed that that was his own opinion. Not to be mixed up with officialdom. Mr Hyde would come through when going through the official rules. This long phone conversation ended with his pleading with me not to give up as England needed good teachers. I thought they were creating opportunity. But they must have been creating it elsewhere.

What about the survey? They sent me a reply envelope and a form. They asked for a number at which I could be contacted for a telephone interview. I obligingly filled the form in and sent it off. I did want to help the Customer Focus Team in their project of focusing on customers. They so much wanted to hear my views about the standard of service provided, and I so much wanted to give them that information. They so much wanted to develop their procedures and practices to better meet the needs of customers. They so much wanted to do all that. So much so, that the last scene of all, that ends this strange eventful story, was that they forgot to phone me!

The Training and Development Agency for Schools also carried out a survey. The Agency heralded the news by buying up big expensive advertising spaces in The Observer and The Sunday Times. By deducing that the Teacher Training Agency was no longer around, then the tda must be the TTA (remember the roadshow?) in a glittery new dress. The advertisement went like this:

"The Training and Development Agency for Schools has been asked by the Secretary of State for Education and Skills to review the standards for classroom teachers. The aim of this review is to achieve a more coherent set of standards, which will establish clear career pathways. This should enable you and your colleagues to identify better, more focussed professional development, helping you maximise your career potential. The standards under review are the existing standards for QTS, Induction, Senior Teacher (threshold) and Advanced Skills

Teacher. In addition, we are developing standards for the Excellent Teacher Scheme. You have the opportunity to influence the content of these standards."

and then they ask teachers to complete their online questionnaire.

So, are tda saying that TTA were unsuccessful in
1) establishing coherent standards
2) establishing clear career pathways
3) assisting teachers in identifying and focusing on professional development
4) maximising teachers' career potential?

If teachers are professionals, why are all these overhead activities needed?

On 25th September 2005, The Observer published an article about state education in Finland. The article claimed that since the OECD's first major education study, in 2000, Finland has led the world in literacy, and its 15 year olds are the best at solving maths. The headteacher of Arabia School, the best school in the world, claimed that the reason for their success lies in their teachers. Teachers are highly regarded by the authorities and trusted by the authorities to find the best solutions in their job.

30

And, now we come to my second Comprehensive. This time it was temporary cover. I was going to share the job with another newly-employed teacher. I lived in hope that my first Comprehensive was an exception. I would soon find out that the pattern of state education repeats itself frequently all over the country.

I was interviewed by the deputy head and the head of English. They both seemed competent men. But I was overly impressed by the head of English, who I'll refer to as Peter. Peter was a young man in his early thirties, he had an aura of confidence about him, someone who had a firm grip on his job, really on the ball. It was quite a big Comprehensive and he had all that responsibility bestowed on him. That evening, I told my friend what an enterprising and brilliant individual Peter was. I was soon to find out otherwise.

Peter was always exhausted. At first, I worried so much about him that I wondered whether I should speak to the deputy head about Peter being close to a nervous breakdown. Peter couldn't give me much attention, he said, because of the school play. "Just keep the lid on it for me, Anna. Thanks".

The difference between this school play and one I had seen performed at the independent school was vast, as different as night is from day. This school play was more self-absorbed tomfoolery than anything else. It was youngsters playing themselves. The play at the independent school had been a musical and, without exaggeration, it was worthy of the West End. I simply couldn't believe how brilliant the performance was. Gripped throughout. Astonishing choreography, flamboyant costumes, real ability to sing, dance and act out the most diverse characters.

31

I soon came into contact with Year 9 (13-14 year olds). It was like being in hell without the fun. Devoutly not to be wished on anyone. This was a rural area and there was an interesting mix of children. The school was within commuting distance of London. Therefore, children of affluent business people attended a school which had originally been built for a rural village. Also, a large council estate had been built within the school's catchment area. Classes were pieced together with children from these three backgrounds. In my Year 9, apart from the way they talked, the children's attitude to ponies said a lot about them. The eloquent daughters of the London business people boasted about getting ponies for their birthdays or as a Christmas present. They tied coloured bows wherever they could on them and called them names like Pixie or Shelley. The rustically spoken didn't know how many ponies they had, whilst the council estate kids, who varied their sentences by gracing every other one with an "F" word, couldn't have given a toss about ponies.

It was at this school where the roads of arrogance and ignorance met. The arrogance mostly came from the commuter kids. One such girl stomped into the classroom late one day, slammed the door and snatched a photocopy from my hand as she walked past me to go to her place. These kids knew more about teaching than teachers. One day, they would make great teacher trainers. One commuter girl crept up behind me while I was writing on the whiteboard and rubbed out part of what I had written, an estate girl removed an overhead transparency while it was being projected, and I was discussing the contents, and the rurals would crumple or tear up handouts promptly upon receipt.

When books needed handing out the rurals whirled them onto desks or threw them at pupils causing a loosening of the binding, with covers coming off. They had even broken a desk and rendered it unfit for use. I knew exactly what a colleague meant when she complained that we teachers were considered little more than servants by children and parents alike. Parents sided with children against teachers. This may stem from the parents' denial of having failed to provide their children with adequate moral boundaries. With a hint of envy, the teacher reminisced how all her university friends, who had gone into teaching, had left the profession. They were earning a damn sight more than her and, moreover, living it up in their free time while she was at home marking. She, too, was seeking to flee.

My Year 11 (15 to 16 year olds) was a top group. They would be taking GCSE English at the end of the school year. I was amazed how little effort they put into their work. Hardly any of them carried out the homework I set. I had already set four essay assignments. Out of twenty-nine pupils, only three had handed in every piece of work. Every single pupil did her homework at the independent school. When report time came around at this Comprehensive, under 'Suggestions for Improvement', I decided to write that doing one's homework was an excellent method for improvement and also stated how many pieces of homework were missing.

One particular girl, who I'll call Pam, had handed in nothing, like many others in the class. Pam's father sent me a letter which I found in my pigeon hole. This father was livid that his daughter had been accused of laxity. And, it transpired that Pam was totally ignorant as to what the homework could be about! Would I please send him a list of all the assignments set?! On the same day, Pam handed in all her outstanding homework. What was I to answer? I sent him a list of the homework and wrote that, on the same day I received his letter, his daughter had handed all the work in and back dated it. Therefore, I concluded Pam knew exactly what the homework entailed. No apology came back. So, there I was trying hard to help his daughter and that's how my efforts were received.

Although he got the wrong end of the stick, at least he bothered. I thought that when parents saw my comments, they would be up in arms about their kids not doing their homework. I naively thought they would back me up. I had visions of essays coming at me from all directions. Nothing like that happened, unfortunately. Apart from Pam's father, total silence. I told Peter about this. He said that you can't force them. Anyway, why was I setting essays? I should stop that. Rather than telling them about poems and novels, I should be making them do research and they would then present their findings to the class each lesson. That way they would do the lesson preparation themselves, saving the teacher from doing it. If students hadn't got anything ready, they would have to improvise. Alternatively, students could be put in groups and discuss what they had prepared. Those within the groups who hadn't done their preparation could just listen. I answered that I didn't agree with him. Firstly, it's no good listening to the viewpoints of those who know as much, or less, than yourself. You need someone to give you a broader view. After that, discussion can ensue with the class. Furthermore, their opinions could then be expressed individually in their essays, in writing. What was wrong with sitting in a quiet corner at home, collecting their thoughts and opinions and writing them down in good clear English? And, surely they had to get a lot of essay writing practice before their exams. Otherwise, how would they manage? No, I was totally wrong.

Another piece of advice from him, which left me agog, was that I shouldn't bother correcting spelling or grammar mistakes - it took too long. Moreover, it was hardly of any use because in the GCSE exam students were not marked down on spelling and grammar, except on one piece and not many points were at stake anyway. Results were King. Anything else was a waste of time and effort. One day he suggested that I simply let them speak amongst themselves about anything they liked, rather than teaching them anything, because they were all so tired. Why didn't they just all stay at home in bed in that case?

In all honesty, the kids didn't like my approach because up till then, apart from coursework and mock exams, they hadn't been asked to write essays and they thought their grammar and spelling were great. I think I came to them like a thunderbolt. With hindsight, I remember that they had an incredulous look on their faces when I set the first essay assignment for homework. I didn't think anything of it. But to them it must have sounded like someone had just asked them to climb Everest and K2 simultaneously. With time, they started getting used to me and essays started trickling in. One girl, in particular, improved enormously. She was not of the best. In fact, she'd got a D in her mock exams. She came to me one day on her own and said she was going to strive to get an A. I had told them they could all get an A. All they had to do was work hard for it because they were intelligent kids. This particular girl wrote five essays and the difference between her first and fifth was enormous.

We were getting on well until one day just before a lesson with Year 11, a member of my family was taken ill. I had to go home immediately. My class sat in with Peter's class who was teaching the same novel. Various students were asked to comment on one page of the novel in front of the class. The next lesson my students told me they didn't like that approach. However, Peter insisted that I change my method to his. In fact, he was now coming to sit in one of my lessons. He admitted that my knowledge of Literature was admirable but the approach of lecturing them, then discussing, then writing, was wrong. I had to do it his way: no lecturing, no writing, just discussions initiated by them. For the rest of the time I was there, I ignored him, like the other teachers did, and continued to do exam preparation my way. As professionals teachers should be trusted with what they are doing.

32

Let's look at the definition of professional. Professionals have a vast array of skills and experience. They are able to exercise judgement about any situation in their profession and are able to apply the correct skill to that situation. What are teachers in England today? People who do exactly what they are instructed to do by an internal or external authority. People who should take exactly the prescribed time over tasks and keep extensive records, so that authorities can satisfy themselves that teachers have complied with all their requirements. People who have value judgements imposed on them undermining their authority and who are deemed not having good judgement, therefore not trusted.

If further evidence is needed that teachers are bottom of the heap, one can simply glance at the statement of political policy, which the Blair government intends to follow, called the Schools' White Paper issued on 25th October 2005. In its more than 100 pages, "teachers" and "teaching" obtain 230 counts in total, while "parents" clock up 444 (!)

The "professionals" according to the White Paper, are the parents. Parents, or anyone who is prepared to put up money, can get involved in the provision of schools. Not only. Parents will be able to found new schools! Along with all this a shiny new bureaucracy, called the Schools' Commissioner, is to be created with "dedicated choice advisors" ever at the ready.

As an analogy, let's suppose that parents took over a dental practice which treated children's teeth in a given area. Parents could have the choice of having their children's teeth filled with, let's say, self-adhesive resin cement (SARC) or with resin modified glass ionomers (RMGI). Choice is good. The mother can just tell the dentist she wants SARC for her boy, who we'll call Toby. After the mother has chosen the best drill for the job, the dentist can go ahead. Let's suppose though that the next 29 children have to accept SARC as well because it is mixed in portions of 30. Let's suppose that one of those 30 is my child, and I want her teeth filled with RMGI. What happens? Do all the children have SARC because the other mother is more bolshy than me? Do we vote? Do we call up the "dedicated choice advisors"?

When everything is set up, the next step is to take Toby to the dentist. His mother has fed him on trash all his life. The holes in his teeth are like craters. So, she complains to the dentist about the dire state of Toby's mouth. The dentist answers that it will take a lot of sittings to get this mouth right. The mother heads home and leaves the dentist to it.

While his mother is away, Toby obstinately locks his jaws. The dentist would like to wrench Toby's mouth open but fears being sued. The dentist spends ample time in coaxing Toby into opening his mouth, but to no avail. No, Toby's mouth is a vice. All of a sudden Toby opens his mouth, swears at the dentist, and locks it again. The other 29 are waiting around for the dentist to finish with Toby. They get bored, so they start taking the waiting room apart and hitting each other. The dentist decides to give up on Toby and tries to stop the other 29 children from wrecking the joint. It's four o'clock, the children go home and my girl's teeth do not get filled. In fact, nobody's teeth are filled. In fact, it has been a waste of a day.

That evening, Toby tells his mother that the dentist picked on him and didn't do any work at all on his teeth. The next day the mother decides to go back down to the practice and give the dentist a piece of her mind! How dare he pick on her child! "Go and pick on someone your own size. It's a good job my husband hasn't heard about this, or he'd have come down here like a shot. My George doesn't hang around, you know!" The unhappy episode comes to a climax when the dentist seeks to defend himself by saying that Toby wouldn't open his mouth. The mother sees red. "Toby didn't open his mouth because you bored him stiff! What kid wants its teeth filled by a dentist as boring as you?" How dare he not offer extra-curricular fun activities to keep her Toby happy? Having teeth filled is so distant from everyday life. How could Toby identify with the activity? If the practice had been more like a fairground, Toby would have been more than happy to open his mouth. The dentist is kicked out without further ado and a new one is sought.

* * *

An advert appears in the Times Dental Supplement:

For a Designated Specialist practice with 'Leading Edge Status', parents wish to appoint, a dynamic, energetic, enthusiastic and forward-looking SARC specialist to fill children's teeth from Year 7 to Year 11.

This progressive practice has State of the Art facilities. It is exciting, heavily over-subscribed and will run a dense programme of extra-curricular life relevant fun activities. We are equipped with

TV/Video, and access to modern ICT facilities on a pleasant site. The practice has Beacon Status. Number on roll: 173+.

This practice has a long tradition of superb fillings within a friendly and supportive community. We have 'Investors in People' status and we participate in the Open Door Dental Scheme every year. We are highly regarded for our value-added achievement.

Teeth First applicants are welcomed. Immediate start. (Pay spine and 'Golden Hello'). We are committed to the promotion of equality, social justice and excellence.

Upon receipt of a full length letter of application and detailed CV, candidates will be sent a specially tailored recruitment pack, including application form and complete completion instructions. Please state what other activities you can offer as well as dentistry, and send us the names, addresses and telephone numbers of two referees. CRB enhanced clearance required.

* * *

After interviewing several promising candidates, parents finally decide upon a young dentist who, among his other credentials, shows films of mega-galactic creatures drilling mega-galactic canines with laser guns and then filling them using cranes.

Toby's parents have also filled their son's head with trash. Nothing that requires substantial intellectual engagement has passed the threshold of Toby's brain. Concentrating is demanding and takes effort. It's even painful for Toby. Toby is not used to this and can't see the point. So school seeks to emulate society and tries to turn it into a place where fun takes priority. Everyone must give Toby what he likes. What does Toby like? TV, playstation, football, Martians, chocolate, mobile phones, and willies. Somehow, teachers have to motivate Toby by making their subject matter relevant to his likes.

126

Teachers can teach grammar through football, Literature through TV, Religion through chocolate ... the holiday-camp school. If Toby's happy, so are his parents. Of course, Toby also needs to get qualifications. Therefore, GCSEs (and A levels) are structured so that through drilling him, making exams easier and allowing assisted coursework, Toby can get decent grades without learning much at all.

In an article printed on 9th October 2005, in The Sunday Times, it was reported that the government's exam watchdog is worried about cheating in GCSE coursework. Figures from the five exam boards show that 3,600 teenagers were caught breaking the rules in 2004 - nine percent up on the year before. The QCA (Qualifications and Curriculum Authority) will publish results of a two-year investigation into coursework, as well as new rules to crack down on cheating. As part of the inquiry, children were asked to fill in forms confiding how much help they had received. A spokesman at the QCA explained that "Parents helping with coursework is not cheating" but "Parents writing coursework is cheating". You can buy tailor-made essays for about £50.-- off the Internet (on *www.coursework.info* you can sign up for as little as £9.99 and have access to nearly 3,000 English essays). Eventually the QCA will come to the conclusion that coursework will be abolished because it is impossible to stop cheating. It took a two-year investigation to find that out, Lassie could have told the watchdog years ago.

Toby has to get at least five GCSEs because the school needs that result for its league-tables. Rather than harassing Toby by making him think hard, easier subjects are created for Toby, like Food Technology, Leisure, Tourism, Manufacturing and Media. The school goes up the league tables, and with very little knowledge between his ears, Toby can flaunt his pass marks. Everyone's happy.

What use is knowledge anyway? You can find out anything you need through the Internet. In fact, Internet can even replace the brain. Toby does not internalise much because there is no need. He

127

downloads his coursework, homework, research ... you name it and Toby knows where to find it. Why bother memorising it all? On this note, according to an IT publication, IEEE Spectrum, "polymer nanowires threaded through the bloodstream may be a practical way to enter the cranium". Dow Jones state that the ultimate goal "is to have a direct wire into our brains to have complete knowledge of who we are and what makes us tick...". Maybe parents will be able to wire their little ones up and get them through GCSEs and A levels that way! No strain, no pain.

In the meantime, parents must take responsibility for their children's education. Parents who persist in actually educating their children are not yet extinct! These parents create a lifestyle which is congenial to learning. All the children I taught at the independent school were members of such families. Let's call one of these children Lizzy. To start off with Lizzy's house has lots of books in it, including various dictionaries. Lizzy also regularly goes to the local library with her grandmother. Her parents find time to discuss what she's reading. Lizzy is taken to art exhibitions, museums and country houses. And she talks to her family about what she sees. Lizzy even goes to the theatre or a concert from time to time. At a Summer School I attended, one of my English tutors told our class that his mother had taken him to see <u>Richard III</u> when he was six. Though he was about 45 at the time and lecturing in Literature at Cambridge, he said it was the performance of a Shakespeare play that had had the most impact on him and which he remembered with the greatest pleasure. Compare that to Toby's parents. Culturally speaking, what have they given their son?

Trash TV. Toby has ended up in a vortex of strong easy-to-understand images. They seem to fill his life with excitement. But, they make him passive. They show him a life which distorts reality and turns his brain into bread-and-butter pudding. Responsible parents realise the negative effects most TV programmes and adverts have and will protect their children from them. Yes, it is difficult to be different. Much easier to share the common values of those surrounding us and conform. Commercial TV makes money by taking over Toby's brain and degrading it. If people give importance to trash TV and buy the products advertised, how can higher values be instilled in Toby?

That's where parent power lies: switching off the TV and imprinting the joy of learning on a child's mind from the word go. That way, parents will hand over a teachable child to teachers. Lizzy's parents have a totally different mindset from Toby's parents and they pass their outlook, and capability to think, on to their daughter. When I presented <u>Midsummer Night's Dream</u> to Year 8 (12-13 year olds) at the independent school, some of the children already knew the play and had even seen a performance! They got very excited and clapped their hands when they heard we were going to study the play. Teachers are handed Tobies and Lizzies. If Lizzy's parents can afford it, even if it means forgoing holidays, they will send Lizzy to an independent school. Teachers can actually teach there. Having worked in both the state and independent sectors in England, based on my experience, if parents can possibly afford it, they would do well to send their children to an independent school. Although, education begins at home.

The government will insist that it is trying to compensate for the differences between Toby and Lizzy. Holiday-camp school is doing Toby no favours. By making it easy and bending over backwards for him, we are not giving him what he needs. We are not giving him the possibility to catch up with Lizzy. Lizzy will make it in the world of work anyway. Apart from the connections her parents might have, attending an independent school means investing in networking. Toby might have the grades, but he hasn't really been taught to write or speak properly. He hasn't been allowed to acquire an inquiring mind, he knows little about grammar, his spelling is atrocious, and he cannot construct an argument or structure a discussion. Sound writing skills are the fruit of years of reading and thinking. It doesn't happen at a holiday-camp. It doesn't even mean you have these abilities because you have a GCSE or an A level in English. There are no shortcuts.

A horrible thought, maybe outrageous, has struck me. Has the government a secret grand plan to turn our future generations into uncritical thinkers and incompetent communicators, so that they can be easily manoeuvred? No, can't be.

33

Back to school. My tutor group was a Year 7. This class practically destroyed the classroom. The lack of maintenance at the school did not make teachers' lives easier. I never found out what the caretaker looked like. Call me distracted. I could not leave anything in the classroom without fear that it would get removed or destroyed. To add to the mayhem, the classroom had been appointed a tutor base. It meant that children could use the classroom as a living-room during breaks. After breaks, the place was strewn with litter, crisp bags, empty bottles, sweet wrappers were all over the floor. These went to add to the crumpled handouts, paper airplanes, broken pencils, and upturned chairs already on the floor. Sometimes, there would even be upturned desks. That's when you noticed just how much chewing gum they stuck under the desks. I'd have to pick at least some of the litter up before starting the following lesson. It didn't all fit in the wastepaper bin, anyway, it overflowed, the place was a tip. One day some kids had stood on the desks and had removed some foam tiles from the classroom's ceiling.

Apart from all this, any piles of books would be knocked over, material would be taken out of cupboards and scattered about or moved. How was that the fault of the caretaker, then? I thought the caretaker might go round the school and see what needed fixing. Nothing could be locked up in the classroom. There was an old filing cabinet behind the teacher's desk which had no keys for the lock. There were three drawers in the desk and no keys for the lock. There was a metal cabinet and keys for the lock, but the lock was broken. There were keys to the classroom door, but the lock was broken as was the door handle. The door did not even close. Kids would run by in the corridor while lessons were in progress, kick the door wide open and run off. The metal door knob would cause a clang against the metal cupboard standing right behind it. The loud metallic sound would reverberate in the classroom and the kids in the class would take this as a sign to make even more noise by squealing. Some kids added a variant to their hit and run technique. They would hurl an object into the classroom. We once were the target of balloons filled with water. The kids would also bring wads of mud into the classroom on a wet day. They would pick bits off their wads and throw them at each other. This was no place to wear Armani.

34

One day during the break I was busy picking up chocolate wrappers and crisp packets. At first, I didn't notice. But, in the direction of the door, out of the corner of my eye, I thought I saw Philip Larkin looking in. He disappeared suddenly. Was this a vision or a waking dream? Had Philip Larkin come back from the grave to haunt me? To bring me a message? Maybe he had come to tell me that I had been overly optimistic about English state education. Expected too much. "A good dose of pessimism, that's what you need, old girl". Yes, that must have been his message. What else could it be? Unless he had come to straighten out the library.

I rushed to the door just in time to see him go down the corridor and disappear into Peter's classroom. No, it wasn't Philip Larkin, no bicycle clips.

One of the other English teachers came in to tell me he was an inspector. "Poor man, he looks so miserable", I commented. No sooner said than he re-appeared at the door again, accompanied by Peter. This time the inspector found it in him to utter "Good morning". Yes, it was a beautiful morning; I thought he hadn't noticed. Peter told me that this man would sit in my next lesson. "Very well", I answered. Not too fussed.

In twenty-five years' teaching in Switzerland, I'd only undergone two inspections at two different institutions. That was it. Headteachers knew who the good teachers were. In the time I had taught in England, inspections were so frequent that I was getting used to people poking their noses in. There are no classroom assistants in Swiss state schools. How do teachers manage? First of all, class sizes are smaller. Then, the really badly behaved children are sent to special independent schools. For example, one boy's parents were invited to remove their child from state school. He was ruining learning for other children and was a bad role model for the others. The headteacher suggested they take him to a nearby school run by a religious foundation. Who pays the fees? The Swiss state pays most of the fees. Anyway, these schools are nowhere near as expensive as English independent schools. They serve a different purpose. Teachers don't need degrees when the priority is teaching problematic students to behave well. I suppose the teachers in those schools are on a par with teaching assistants in England. You have to be realistic, an academic would be absolutely frustrated in a school like that.

You may be wondering about all those expensive Swiss colleges. They are mostly for foreigners. Children whose parents don't want to, or can't, send their children to school in their own country. Although all schools have their problems, these are excellent schools rather like the Swiss state schools for natives, and the schools in the independent sector in England.

We've talked a lot about badly behaved children but what about those who simply can't keep up? There again, the Swiss system is different. Weaker children don't continue with the syllabus like the rest. If a teacher believes that the child has been struggling, the child will repeat the year. Once the child has caught up, s/he can proceed to the next stage. In one class, it's quite usual to find children of different ages. A child of seven can be as bright as a child of nine. I am going off at a tangent, I'd like to get back to Philip Larkin's double.

It was break-time, so he told me he'd be back. He must have gone off to get a strong cup of tea and read the Daily Telegraph. While he was away, the other English teacher gave me some hints. First of all, he likes to see dictionaries on desks, one for each student. I should start with a five-minute warm up, I was told. So I combined the two with a starter of five minutes' dictionary work. Then I thought I'd get the children to draw up a survey. After that, they would use their sheets to carry out a research project amongst their classmates. Finally, they would report their findings to the class. Yes, I had it all sussed out. It was the kind of lesson inspectors liked. But it wasn't going to be easy. This was the class that persuaded one teacher to choose early retirement. She said teaching had never been as bad as it was in that year. She had reached the limit.

The lesson started well. The children were a little intimidated by the inspector at first, but they soon relaxed. When the children started drawing up the survey, I went to the classroom assistant who had beckoned me over. She told me that she would have to leave right away because she was accompanying a group of older children on a theatre outing. She left saying that they were all behaving much better than usual and the lesson was going well.

When I turned around, two of the children sitting directly in front of the inspector, had slid under their desks and had started eating crisps in full view of the inspector. I got them out, made them put their crisps away and get on with their work. While I was doing that, two other boys ran out into the corridor ranting. I went to the door and a colleague happened to be passing. I asked her if she would take care of them for the rest of the lesson because I had the inspector observing and my classroom assistant had had to leave. She obligingly agreed.

So back to the lesson. I got the children to carry out their surveys then some came out to the front of the class and reported their findings. It all went smoothly in the end. The children left. The inspector was not happy. He said the behaviour was unacceptable. He didn't know that they had behaved much better than usual!

35

In the staff room, you could overhear talk of the children's problematic lives. Nearly every kid who behaved like a monkey had an excuse for doing so. No-one thought of looking at what was positive in their lives and tried to link that to reasons why they should behave well. Lists were handed round to teachers indicating what problem each kid was afflicted with. At least fifty percent were included in the list. The Special Needs teacher was busily nit-pickingly bringing the negatives to the surface resulting in pleas for clemency. I once read an article written by an African teacher who had come to England to teach in a comprehensive. He was shocked by the bad behaviour and claimed that he came from a third world country, but it was England which had third world education. He walked out after only a few days. Why don't African children behave as badly given that they are deprived?

The Special Needs teacher came at me with all sorts of maladies and acronyms I'd never come across. Some kids suffered from ADD and she gave me a list of those afflicted by it. Having come from abroad, she did not think that I might not know what ADD is. A kind of obsession with putting things together? An exaggeration by increment? Totalling up everything in sight?

No, of course, it was Attention Deficit Disorder. Surely, the disorder could not have been new. They had simply given it a local habitation and a name and raised it to the heights of something serious. We simpletons of years past remember it as daydreaming. We were those little naive romantics who invited clips around our ear for staring into thin air or stubbornly fixing our gaze on our ink-wells, or for looking out of the window across the playing field at Archibald in his long-johns. A quick clip and concentration was regained. What was the DCRR (daydreaming clip reality regained) sequence must have turned into ADD.

One child in Year 9 was particularly disruptive. To protect his identity, I shall call him Tom. I don't know if Tom was afflicted by some malady, or if he was simply rude, that is, if the adjective still exists to refer to school children's behaviour. Tom would come in swearing, jeering and knocking over anything that was on his way. While I was trying to explain something to the class, he would suddenly shout across the room drowning my voice. He was usually late. Because of this he would have to perch on the end of someone else's desk given that there were thirty children in the class and only fourteen desks. Each desk was for two students. This was a tiny classroom and more desks simply would not fit into the space. To have thirty children huddled together like that does not make a teacher's life easier. The maximum number of children to a class in Switzerland is twenty-five. However, the maximum was rarely reached. I would usually have about eighteen, sometimes more. But never did three pupils have to share a desk meant for two.

On 14th September 2005, the Daily Mail wrote that a report was issued in which it was revealed that despite average spending per student, at primary level, the UK has one of the largest class sizes. There are around 26 pupils in primary school classes compared to an OECD average of 21.6. Only Turkey, Japan and South Korea have

larger classes and in all but nine countries there are between 16 and
21.

36

Peter had the bottom group for Year 9 (13-14 year olds). Tom should obviously have been in Peter's class, maybe he wasn't wanted there. In other subjects, they must have got the mix right because the problem kids were only all together for English and, quite coincidentally, all in my class.

One day it got so bad that I called for the headteacher in order to get Tom, together with another two children, removed from the lesson. The headteacher couldn't have come soon enough to the scene. When he did arrive, he told the class that if they didn't behave decently, they wouldn't do well in their national tests. He looked at Tom, and the boy gave the headteacher some cheek, too. The headteacher decided to give them another chance and not remove them from the lesson. So they carried on as before. The headteacher disappeared from sight leaving me to sort it out.

Peter heard about the episode and said he would take the boy into his class during the afternoon's Drama lesson. At the beginning of that lesson, I asked the boy to accompany me, to Peter's classroom. Surprisingly, Tom, quite obediently, did as he was told. Upon arrival, we were greeted with: "Sorry, but I can't possibly do this, Tom's got to stay with you. Thanks". So back we traipsed to the drama studio. There were high blackened windows in the studio which had wide windowsills. Tom decided he'd like to stand on one of them. When I sought to get him down, he would walk along the ridge, pivot and walk back. A girl took it upon herself to switch all the lights off and we were left in total darkness. Boys started howling and girls screaming. As Yeats would have said "Mere anarchy is loosed upon the world".

37

During one of the following lessons, some girls in Year 9 got a packet of fruit flavoured condoms out of their bags, blew them up and threw them around the classroom. A few days later, I found out that one of these girls had been suspended for sending extremely obscene text messages to her friends. In the staff room, I had overheard that one girl in Year 11 was pregnant and teachers were worried that she might opt out of exams.

In assembly one day, the centrepiece was a sermon on sexuality given by a science teacher. According to this senior teacher giving the sermon, England had more teenage pregnancies than any other country in the Western world because we didn't talk enough about sex. She was perfectly convinced that we were repressed. In formulating her philosophy, she surmised that in order to improve the situation, we should talk about sex more. We needed to get our inner-most feelings expressed and shared. The statistics showed that English teenagers were doing that alright!

Quite by coincidence, the day before, I'd read a newspaper article which claimed the contrary: teenage pregnancies were due to too much liberalism in discussing sex. The opinion was that sex should not be scrutinised too much because it makes teenagers want to experiment. After they'd done that, they would usually decide they would like to continue exploration. Weighing up theoretical sex and physical sex on scales, why did one have to plummet while the other went soaring up? What about moderation? What about telling the kids that they have feelings they are not allowed to follow? Doesn't the same go for drinking, smoking, taking drugs, swearing, and behaving with disrespect, too? Most things were granted to these kids, and they took. Too many of their demands were met while no sense of duty was instilled in them to counterbalance it all. A very out-dated argument.

38

One day, some girls from my tutor group (Year 7, 11-12 years old) came to talk to me in the classroom over lunchtime. Most of the girls complained about the long stretches of time spent on their own at home. Some had to let themselves in after school and maybe look after younger siblings.

One girl told us that the first thing she did when she got home after school was to make tea for herself and her younger brother. Then they'd watch TV or play computer games until their mother came home three hours later. She added that being home without an adult frightened her. The sense of loneliness was easily captured in her words. What shocked me most, though, was what they said next. They had all been drunk before. They found it incredible that I had never got drunk. "You must have done, Miss, for your birthday". "No, not even for my birthday, I tell you". An impossibility commensurate with my never having breathed. Loneliness sought to be overcome by strong sensations. Again no sense of measure.

Leaving children on their own and then compensating by giving in to their whims destabilises children. Boredom ensues from a lack of a sense of purpose. Children become frustrated when their wishes are not met and can become aggressive. This sense of boredom and the lack of self-control stems from unclear moral restrictions and leads to their not recognising authority and challenging anyone who represents authority. Teachers represent authority. The concessions made to children for their difficulties make them consider themselves helpless victims and also releases them from taking responsibility for their actions. Their scapegoats are adults.

Adults deny children a sense of community and this increases the feeling of emptiness and insecurity which is sometimes filled with an excess of sex, drugs and alcohol. The glue of community has lost its hold and compact neighbourhoods are disappearing. Church is being attended less and less. Local greengrocers are being replaced by soulless hypermarkets. Milkmen hardly do the rounds any more.

Traditional values are fading out and no valid alternatives are replacing them.

Children have easy access to television. The media distort and amplify reality and youngsters, who are trying to find their way in the world, are the easiest to manipulate. They are caught in a virtual wonderland in which the pace is set by the least suitable and most able. The more our society becomes complex and sophisticated, the more young people become fragile as does the instability of a system, such as that of the disintegration of the extended family, not to mention the nuclear family.

Children have difficulty finding role models and identifying with adults. The turnover of teachers in English comprehensives is astronomical. You only need to visit the TES Website to see how many vacancies there are. The teachers in Switzerland tend to stay put for years. It is usual for older teachers to have the sons and daughters of former pupils in their classes. Children get attached to teachers and wonder why a teacher abandons them to go to another school. In the UK, it is easier to get promotion and go up the salary scale, if teachers school hop.

39

Back to my Comprehensive. Fridays were dedicated to religious assembly and a vicar would be shipped in. Most of the time the voice didn't carry to the whole hall so, apart from the first few rows, you could hardly capture the gist of the sermon. This led to kids fidgeting and whispering to friends. However, one day, we did get an interesting assembly and the lady vicar came over loud and clear. Her sermon was about the relationship between God and chocolate. I would have thought that this casual comparison would contribute little to advancing the esteem owed to God in the eyes of the world. She had, she said, been eating chocolate and reading the wrapper (an intellect by teacher training standards) when it occurred to her that the words printed were heresy. The gist of the meaning was that this chocolate was the best thing you could ever come across. Which, of course, it wasn't. God was. I would have thought that they each served different purposes, otherwise why should she be eating the chocolate rather than getting her fill of God?

No-one had told the vicar that it was a mere marketing technique and wasn't expected to be taken literally. Those who wrote the slogan most probably thought that sex was better than chocolate, but they didn't write that on the chocolate wrapper! It is true that advertising gurus come up with such turns of phrases which offend the intelligence of most people. But to the vicar it was a ploy to belittle God. The terrible consequence was that in some cases the vicar's argument backfired. Kids were beginning to think that chocolate was as good as God. One girl in my class brought a parody of the Lord's Prayer in the worship of chocolate. Such grand lines as "Give us today our daily e-numbers".

One of the most astounding changes which had taken place in the years I had been away from England was the importance that chocolate wrappers had acquired in education and religion. Not even the Swiss, whose chocolate is second to none, had thought of the many uses one of their most sublime products could be put to. One of the reasons is that Swiss chocolate is not wrapped in empty rhetoric. The quality of the chocolate speaks for itself. Intellectual teacher trainers are starved of material to psychoanalyse teachers with, while vicars can't draw gooey comparisons. So what happens to chocolate wrappers in Switzerland? They are thrown in the bin.

40

My Year 10 (14 to 15 years old) was a bottom group. Before I had ever met them, I had heard horror stories about them. Some were in this bottom group because their behaviour was not quite Prince of Wales. Others were there because they couldn't string one sentence together on 'My Day at the Zoo'. It was the first time, that I witnessed two students seriously fighting in class. Even Year 7 (11-12 years old) children would thump each other when they got the chance.

These two boys started hurling verbal abuse at each other and in no time at all one suddenly strode across to the other, knocking chairs over on the way, and delivered hearty blows to the other. The victim reacted by thumping back, so a boxing-cum-wrestling match ensued to the glee of the rest of the class who enjoyed the show. Just like the wild west. Of course, I called management. Because I insisted, this time the trouble-makers were removed from the classroom.

Of the others in the class, those who had made an effort to write a fair deal, I would reward by letting them go to the computer room to type their work up. This encouraged them to engage in work. Four of the calmer ones had made a great effort, so I asked the IT teacher if it was possible for them to use the computers during the following lesson. The IT rooms were just across the corridor. One room was free. Rightly enough, the teacher didn't want disruptive children in the computer room. I gave him the names of the boys. He was certain they would behave well so gave me his permission. Before the four went off to the computer room, I warned them about their behaviour. Their absence from class also gave me more time to dedicate to the weakest.

I sat with one of the most disruptive boys in the class and tried to coax some ideas out of him. Then I asked him to write them down by dictating to him. My heart sank when I realised that the boy couldn't write. He tried but only scrawl came out of his pen. His letters were enormous and unsteady, and although he was writing on lined paper, his lines plummeted downwards on the page. He was fifteen and wrote like a three-year-old. It was very sad. This boy was practically illiterate. He didn't have a snowball's chance in hell of obtaining even a shadow of a GCSE. How was it that all the adults who had surrounded him up till then had abandoned him to himself? No wonder he sat at the back of the class talking about wanking all the time.

Wanking was an obsession of his. He wound the others in the class up with his dirty talk. Sometimes, to render the idea, he would undo his zip and pull out the corner of his shirt through the opening so as to simulate his penis. Then he'd get up and walk around the classroom, pulling on the shirt corner and making orgasmic noises. Sometimes he would sit there with his shirt corner sticking out until I went over to him to see if I could get him to do some work. He would bellow like a donkey and pretend to come. He counterbalanced his academic weakness by seeking attention and admiration from others for his defiance.

Anyway, under close surveillance, he was coming up with some work. Peter came in to find out about the fighting. He noticed that

149

quite a few boys were missing so asked where they were. He said that under no circumstances were students to leave the classroom. But they were working, yes, actually working, in the computer room, while I'd got champion wanker to put pen to paper. "No, we can't have this". This conversation was taking place in front of the class. His criticism of handling the class in front of the students undermined my authority. He should have spoken to me in private about any differing views he had. He was utterly unaware about the effect of his words. I told him that I had looked through the glass partitioning a few times already. The boys were behaving well. They didn't even notice I was spying on them because they were typing.

Peter went to the computer room and made the boys come back to the classroom. They were furious. They had printed out their work and, one in particular was sad that he hadn't been allowed to finish. He came and showed me his work, proud of what he had achieved, like a child who has to have its mother's acknowledgement for the effort exacted. "I think you've done brilliantly. This is a fantastic start, we'll work on it and turn it into a great piece of work, OK?"

It didn't happen. The four had gone back to their places, the interest had disappeared in an instant. It takes monumental encouragement and tact to persuade weak students to work and only a moment to demolish their motivation.

41

One morning when I had just arrived at school, I was greeted by the headteacher pacing up and down in the corridor outside my classroom. I thought I was going to get strict surveillance now. I greeted him with a "Good morning" and left it at that. Pretended everything was as usual. No doubt, I would be told in due course. No sooner thought than Peter materialised next to my desk.

"Yesterday morning Anna...", he began. The day before had been my day off. I was miles away. Phew! "Yesterday morning, Anna, something serious happened here", he concluded the sentence. "Anna, your tutor group behaved abominably ...". He was freshly whacked, and he'd only just got up! "Anna, your tutor group went berserk. They went wild yesterday morning and in the scuffle one boy slammed the door shut and caught another boy's fingers in the door. The injured boy fainted and had to be taken to hospital". "I'll have a word with them", I promised. I gave them a good ticking off. So they didn't only misbehave when they were under my care. My job sharer must have been having problems, too. I didn't know this for sure. When we had started the job share, I had tried phoning her to make a first contact so that we could exchange ideas and give each

151

other a hand. I could never get through and finally decided to leave my name and number on her voice mail. She never got back to me.

It wasn't long before I heard that she wanted to leave. I took the opportunity to suggest that if she was leaving, and if they found someone who would like to take the job on full-time, I would be willing to step aside. My job-sharer had, apparently, refused to write up reports for her classes saying that she wanted to be considered a supply teacher. Peter was lumbered with the task. How he could write reports for kids he didn't teach, confused me somewhat.

Needless to say, my job-sharer was being paid much more than me, she didn't even complete her own reports and wanted to leave. My low salary was not counterbalanced by job satisfaction. I sat and thought what the good sides to this job were. I had two friendly and bright level-headed colleagues in my department and excellent teaching assistants. Taken individually most of the children were nice, but taken as classes, well ... and management ...

Peter told me that there had been letters of complaint about me from parents. So I went to see the headteacher and asked about the letters. He confirmed that there hadn't been any. If there had, he would have shown them to me, so that I could tell my side of the story. At least this headteacher had the everything-out-in-the-open approach.

42

The teacher on leave, who I was covering for, during that academic year, had been afflicted by depression and had had to take time off. Year 10 themselves had told me how they took pleasure in making her furious. They had even made her cry in the classroom in front of them. The other two English teachers in the department had told me that it was highly unlikely that she would come back and teach full-time. On top of all the stress of teaching, she also had a baby to look after. One day, she came to visit the school with her baby. They were in the staff room. She told me she'd be returning full-time because she needed the money. She had to hold on to her job. I find it very sad that a mother should miss those wonderful first years of her baby's life.

It seems to me that the British outlook, promoted by the government, is that it is fine to be indebted up to your eyeballs. What we used to call debts are now called credit. Some people seem to be buying all sorts of goods they don't need and can't afford. This keeps the economy ticking over and feels like new-found affluence.

I found it frightening that people in England are prepared to borrow thousands and thousands of pounds in order to buy a house. I really couldn't sleep with all that debt over my head. House prices are ludicrous and have been pushed up by people nonchalantly borrowing and buying. There seems to be no resemblance between the actual value of the house and the money paid for it. Money seems to be thrust upon people. I was listening to a radio interview one day. The interviewee was in financial trouble. She was offered the money by a bank, and she took it. She talked as if she were a victim. Easy come, easy go. Shops are full of unbelievable super bargains, in or out of season, and they are open for ever and ever. Even on Sundays. Sacredness has not gone. It has been transferred to the new cathedrals visited on Sundays where people go to the altar of the cash desk to bow their heads and pay.

A colleague told me it had taken her and her husband years of climbing the property ladder until they could afford a house in the plushest part of town. The house had cost them a fortune and, boy, did they feel it. She'd had only one child, she told me, because they couldn't afford any more. She was forced to work full-time to keep the house. In the meantime, however, she had become fed up with teaching and started wishing they hadn't worked themselves into a corner. Her husband's salary was not enough to keep them in the way they had become accustomed to. "What does he do?", I inquired. "He teaches Economics at a university". Well, if he can't get his finances straight, what hope is there for the rest? After making the house prices soar sky-high in England, some go off to the continent, wallet in hand, thinking that everything is dirt cheap. You wonder why the natives are not snapping up all those bargains themselves.

Some parents have got to have everything and transfer this unhealthy outlook on to their children. It would be so much better to live within one's means and spend more time with your children. If you do have money left over, the best thing you can do is to invest it in your child's education.

43

Overspending does not happen at comprehensives though. The lack of money at ground level in education is shocking. At this Comprehensive four classes at Year 9 were all studying <u>Macbeth</u>. But we only had thirty copies of the text. Given that there were about thirty students in each class, and Year 9 lessons took place simultaneously, if my calculations were right, only one class could use the texts. Two classes could use the texts if students shared.

The best was to come. The English department decided to offer Media Studies the following year. We only had two TVs. I even had to take my own board markers from home. The English cupboard was bare. When I asked Peter for board markers, he apologised and went on to explain that they would take about six weeks to get. "The budget for this month has already been spent, Anna", he puffed. I even had to buy my own study guide. I now realised that the other English teachers had been doing miracles on a shoe-string. Teachers were working their guts out and overcoming the obstacles placed in their way.

In spite of badly-run schools, there are teachers who fight through and stick to their guns. In my experience the teachers in the English department were great examples of the upside of state education. Those who go about their daily work with dedication and who seek no glory for themselves. "The growing good of the world", to quote George Eliot again, "is partly dependent on unhistoric acts". They crossed the hurdles of poor management and bureaucracy when they were placed in their way and carried out their work as well as they were allowed to, between one obstacle and another. This was in stark contrast to management, who placed the obstacles.

Peter, so exhausted by this Comprehensive, was about to take himself off to other waters. He had found himself a job as head of English in an even bigger Comprehensive!

44

By the time I left, I became sick of the vulgarity of some of the pupils, poor management, unhelpful parents, the filth in the classroom, nothing ever getting mended, lack of resources, a scant salary and the slowness of the General Teaching Council. Everything seemed ganged up against me. I wasn't ready to put myself through any more humiliation. I didn't have to put myself through any more of this. I decided to give up teaching in England.

There was no point in insisting. I had gone to England with so much enthusiasm but the experience left me disappointed and drained. It was only when I had come out of the tunnel that I realised how depressed I'd been.

The first thing I did when I got back to Switzerland was to go to the town hall to get my residence permit back. When I received my residence certificate, I felt as if a load had been lifted from my stomach. I had never appreciated Switzerland as much as I had at that moment. It was only by leaving that I realised what a wonderful country it was. It took time, but I gradually got myself back together again. My self-esteem was coming back and I started dressing better after I'd let myself go. What I most wanted was to get my health insurance back. I felt safe again.

Epilogue

So how is it that education reflects Blairism and that part of society which has evolved from the state?

George Orwell brilliantly foresaw a police state in 1984. Only his timing was slightly awry: about twenty years too soon. Dissent is harshly stamped out. Those who do not comply will be demoted like Mo Mowlam and Robin Cook. Or, they will be removed like Ken Livingstone and George Galloway. Even an 82-year-old, a member of the Labour party for about sixty years, Walter Wolfgang, was hoisted up by two heavies and thrown out. Why? Because he dared to disagree, by speaking one word: "rubbish", with Jack Straw at the Labour Party Conference in Brighton in 2005. Police banned Mr Wolfgang from returning to the conference (under the authority of the anti-terror laws). The BBC shows less dissent after eliminating Andrew Gilligan and its then director general Greg Dyke because of the Hutton affair. Blair did not attend either Mo Mowlam or Robin Cook's funeral. Aptitude does not count for much if you do not agree with the thought on high. The same pattern applies in education.

On the contrary, friends remain. Even those who are publicly disgraced. They will be put into hibernation for a while and then resuscitated and brought back. Peter Mandelson was brought back into Government after the Home Loan affair, but was forced to resign again two years later after allegations of misconduct. David Blunkett was also brought back into the Cabinet after being obliged to quit for fast-tracking the passport application of his lover's nanny. If you conform, you stay.

Listening to favoured followers is more important than the public's interests. You can have all the talent, suitability, experience and brilliant ideas you like, but if you are not sympathetic to the ruling body, you will be caught up in a vortex of spin and neutralised. On the other hand, insubstantial castles in the air are promoted, if they are built in accordance with the ruling thought. Similarly, some of the government's legislation turns into messes given that it is not logically thought through. You have to accept, or pretend to accept, all initiatives concocted from on high, if you want to stay. The same pattern applies in education.

In his "Politics and the English Language" published in 1946, George Orwell claimed that bullshit was political bullshit. The present government has produced that in great quantity. I was recently given a book entitled "How Mumbo-Jumbo Conquered the World" by Francis Wheen. It strikes great blows to the quacks of empty pretentious language. The inventors of mumbo-jumbo run rife in government offices. Education included. A paradox given that education should serve the purpose of educating students to think for themselves, form their own opinions and exercise intellectual honesty.

Lies are another deceitful use of language. In an article by Mary Ann Sieghart in The Times of 23rd September 2005, the journalist lays out the web of lies David Blunkett spun between journalists of different newspapers. In the interview with Sieghart, Mr Blunkett stated that he did not wish to discuss the Kimberley Quinn affair. He didn't tell Sieghart that he was being interviewed by the Telegraph and that he did talk about Quinn to the Telegraph. Ms Sieghart rang Mr Blunkett and the latter declared that the Telegraph journalist, Ms Thomson, had made up her quotations or recycled ones from before. Making up quotations is a sackable offence in journalism, so Ms Sieghart suggested Mr Blunkett complain to the Telegraph. He didn't. In the meantime, Ms Thomson confirmed that Mr Blunkett had made all these statements about Ms Quinn during his interview. In a subsequent interview with The Independent, Mr Blunkett declared that Ms Thomson had misquoted him. Ms Thomson asked Mr Blunkett for an explanation. He asked her not to worry because he had never told anyone she was making things up. Yet he did tell someone. He had told Ms Sieghart! This is the pattern of behaviour that I found in school management. What is said one day can be denied the next. Rather than apologise or explain, the instinct is to lie.

Another aspect common to both running the country and education is control freakery. The government will get into every nook and cranny of people's lives. The invention of the "respect" crusade is one example. This itself is disrepectful towards the population. The underlying idea is: you do not know how to behave, so we will have to show you. The same principle applies to teachers. Teachers do not know how to go about their work, we will breathe down your neck until you do as we say although we, ourselves, do not have any proof that our methods are valid.

Furthermore, the Respect Unit, headed by Louise Casey, has cost the population £90 million to set up. This is just one example of costly and useless projects which go nowhere. Similarly, useless money wasting projects run rife in education.

Another favourite of this government is overloading people with paper. The creation of work involved in churning out endless paperwork provides jobs for those sympathetic to the system and frustrates the recipients. Teachers are expected to write down just about everything they do. It can be taken for granted that if you haven't written it down, you haven't done it. That is, you are suspected of not doing much, so you need to prove you are working. Prove yourself innocent. Turning justice on its head. Likewise, in society.

Then, of course, there's the schism created between reality and appearance. New Labour projects a wonderful facade. What goes on behind that facade? When the truth hits Blairites in the face, they just wallop it back and coat it with sugar. Are we moving towards a society in which virtue will have the significance of hidden deviousness? The same applies in education.

As for distorting reality, no means can equal TV for its dexterity in the cause. TV has acquired immense power. If you become popular, even for the most inane reasons, you can use the power deriving from that popularity to boost votes for a politician. Votes are power and power is money. This concatenation of events can only come about if initiated by people boosting the viewing statistics by watching those programmes. Ironically, the only people not to benefit from those programmes, in terms of power and money, are the viewers. It is what happens to Toby.

And now we come to insularity. It is like giving Literature one interpretation. I know that we don't like to be told what to do by foreigners. I myself am anti-European community. But we do need to acknowledge that someone, somewhere else, might have got it right. We need to look at successful educational systems abroad and learn from them. The Schools' White Paper is interesting because, apart from a couple of passing mentions, the government has no serious interest in learning from abroad. It is even admitted in the White Paper that England is 27th, out of 30, as far as education of 16-19 year olds is concerned. We know we are lagging behind. Let's do something new about it.

Instead, we keep going over old familiar ground. Change is the best way of covering tracks. Blair's government has turned full circle in the White Paper by going back to the grant maintained system (Government funds bypassing LEAs) it abolished when it came into power in 1997. Labour becomes New Labour and then New New

Labour. Reforms keep coming. The idea is that if you change frequently enough, the errors in the previous reforms cannot be discovered. In other words, let's cover our tracks, then tread the same ground again in different boots. Layers keep piling up and the ground keeps shifting. Likewise, in education.

Old Labour turned into New Labour and we are now into New New Labour. We are now at Keystage 3 of the National Strategy. This is the Pure Orange Juice government reflected in education. Meddling and muddling. This once great nation, with all its will to fight injustice, has grown tired. It has been overcome by a feeling of acceptance that things will never get better. Smile and bear it. Britannia Rules.

The True Friend

A new translation of Carlo Goldoni's classic play *Il Vero Amico*
(to be published late 2006)

Printed in the United Kingdom
by Lightning Source UK Ltd.
110051UKS00001BA/169-171